Nicolette Coleman is an administrator for a local children's charity. This is her first novel, although her short story, 'Puppet Parody' was published in an anthology: 'Sinister; juxtaposing the ordinary with the bizarre' by Writers Anonymous.

Nicolette lives in a South Essex seaside town with her husband and daughters.

SHOUTING IN A VACUUM

To Carol,

Nicolette Coleman

Shouting in a Vacuum

Happy reading

Nicolette Coleman

Vanguard Press

A CIP catalogue record for this title is
available from the British Library.

ISBN 978 184386 446 2

*Vanguard Press is an imprint of
Pegasus Elliot MacKenzie Publishers Ltd.*
www.pegasuspublishers.com

First Published in 2008

**Vanguard Press
Sheraton House Castle Park
Cambridge England**

Printed & Bound in Great Britain

Dedication

This book is dedicated to my husband, Paul, for making me believe that I could do it. To Samantha Lierens, for giving me the tools and courage. To Karen German for her unending support and love, and Paul German for his advice on police matters.

To Mum and Martin for your support and help, and to all the Writers Anonymous team for their encouragement. Also to Candy, Amber and Finette for always being there and giving me ideas.

ONE

The Barbie doll lay out on the lawn all summer. Her hair became entangled with grass and bleached by the sun. The garden furniture and toys were left out on the dry, yellowing lawn for days on end once the family had got used to the idea that it was unlikely to rain any time soon. The sun shone all day, all week, for many months, and every evening when the children came in they were a darker shade of brown. Bonnie felt that the long, hot days were relaxing her, loosening some hard knot which had grown over the years. Even Dan was less stressed as he arrived home during the long warm evenings.

They had booked a family holiday in Lynmouth for the first week in August. The girls were looking forward to a week at the beach. Summer wanted to sunbathe, and secretly hoped to meet a gorgeous boy while she was resting prettily on the sand. Just into her teens, she was suddenly more interested in boys and clothes than spending time with her family. She was getting taller by the day and now at five foot five inches, was taller than her mother. Her hair was dark and curly, her eyes large and brown, and she was slim but shapely. Skye, on the other hand, still small and skinny with straight, brown hair, preferred to be with her parents, and was happy just to swim or play games. She would be moving into her final year of junior school once the new term began in September, and Bonnie was glad of this chance to spend some time with her youngest daughter before the teenage hormones kicked in. Bonnie and Dan were simply hoping for a chance to relax. Once school had finished, Bonnie was occupied washing and ironing clothes, and packing them in the large suitcase which they invariably took away with them. She was anticipating a lovely time, imagining the family on the beach in the sunshine, having a happy time together, picnicking on the sand and never arguing.

The day they set off for their holiday was the day the weather broke. The journey down to Devon was a nightmare of heavy rain and steamed up windscreens. The girls were restless in the back of the car, and the traffic was dreadful. Dan became moodier as the day wore on, and Bonnie was exhausted with the effort of trying to maintain a light-hearted atmosphere. Dan was hardly ever relaxed since he had become a partner in the law firm. If he was not in the office he was in court, and if he was not in court he was in the office, dictating letters to his long-suffering secretary. At home he had become a grouch, his mind often elsewhere. He had been more laid back than usual when the day began, but like most men, he became angry at being stuck in traffic.

Once they arrived in Lynmouth, however, things began to look up. The cottage had a solid fuel cooker in the kitchen, and two cosy bedrooms above. Bonnie explored every nook and cranny, delighting in the smallness of the house. Skye and Summer happily unpacked their belongings, playing their CDs at top volume until Dan shouted at them to turn the sound down. Bonnie deciphered the instructions for the cooker, and started dinner - a simple pasta dish with tomato and olive sauce. Dan uncorked a bottle of wine, and everybody began to feel better. Over dinner they all chatted about how they intended to spend their week. Summer did not admit to wanting to meet boys for fear of annoying her father, but did own up to wanting to sunbathe on the beach and investigate the local shops. Skye loudly proclaimed that she was going to swim in the sea every day, and would collect rocks from the beach to take home to put in her corner of the garden. Dan became expansive after three glasses of Valpolicella and agreed to whatever his girls suggested. Bonnie felt her face growing pink with the wine and the heat from the cooker, but probably also from the pleasure she felt at being with her lovely family on such a pleasant day.

The following morning Bonnie and Dan took the girls to look around the town. They travelled up in the cliff lift to Lynton and looked at all the shops in the area, stopping for lunch at the cliff-top cafe, where Skye and Summer ordered jacket potatoes and milkshakes, and Bonnie and Dan ordered Greek salad and coffee. As they ate their lunch they all looked out at the view, marvelling at the enormous drop down into Lynmouth.

Once they had paid the bill, they travelled back down in the cliff lift to Lynmouth. Walking along, they discovered the putting green and decided to have a game. The girls had a wonderful time trying to keep their balls on the green, and screaming with laughter when Skye accidentally hit her ball onto somebody else's game. Dan could not help being competitive even with his daughters, much to Bonnie's dismay. She watched her husband surreptitiously. He was nearly six feet tall, with dark brown hair which fell over his forehead as he looked down at the ball. He had been stunningly handsome as a young man.

At least, that had been Bonnie's opinion of him when they first met. Now at 41, Dan was still good looking, but no head turner. The putting game ended with Dan as the victor, but Summer had come a fairly close second. Skye sulked a little at coming last, but was easily cheered by the offer of an ice cream. After a while they headed back to the cottage to begin preparations for dinner. They walked back by way of the river Lyn, stopping every now and then to look at something which caught their interest, or for Skye to throw stones into the fast flowing water. Skye was fascinated by the birds which hopped from rock to rock, stopping occasionally to peer into the swirling water. Dan began to talk about the many souvenir shops they had looked into on their way through the town. "Did you notice the shop selling good luck charms?" he asked Bonnie.

She laughed, and nudged him with her elbow. "What do you need good luck for, Mr Taylor?"

"For having to put up with you lot," he laughed, looking down at her, "but seriously, Bonnie, wouldn't you like one of those horseshoes to go over the back door? It would look lovely with the ivy growing round it, and it would remind us of this holiday."

Bonnie smiled at him. For all his bluster and bad temper, Dan was quite sentimental really. "I suppose you'd like to go and get it now, would you?"

Dan grinned at her. "You must have read my thoughts. You don't mind, do you?"

"No, go on, I'll go back and get the dinner started."

Summer decided to go to the shops with Dan rather than run the risk of having her mother ask her to help with dinner, and so the pair of them set off.

As Bonnie and Skye crossed over the bridge, Bonnie noticed a man walking on the other side of the river. He was watching them closely, and every time they stopped, the man stopped too. Bonnie found this a little peculiar, but decided to ignore him, and once they were back at the cottage, she forgot all about him.

The following two days were drizzly and cool. Summer was moping because she couldn't sunbathe, so Dan took them all back to the putting green to try and better their scores. On the third day Summer improved enough to beat Dan, which cheered her up immensely. When the game was over, Summer decided to go back to the cottage to read her book, while Bonnie, Dan and Skye walked down to the beach. The rain had stopped for the moment, and Skye and Bonnie clambered over the enormous rocks which littered the beach. Skye was dressed in faded blue jeans, with a large hole in the right knee, a blue and white striped T-shirt, and on her head she wore her baseball cap, which she never took off these days. Every so often she had to stop to push the peak up in order that she could see where she was going. Some rocks were so huge that they had trouble climbing onto them, but they laughed and chatted as they clambered up. Dan stood on the beach, hands on hips, looking worried.

"Be careful," he called, "It will be slippery up there."

"We're fine," Bonnie laughed, "don't worry".

"The tide might suddenly come in and cut you off," Dan called back. "You don't know the tides here."

"Worryguts," Bonnie called back, which made Skye giggle.

Dan walked off up the beach and began skimming stones across the sea. Bonnie watched him for a moment, wishing he could relax more. Skye called to her and she turned back. Skye was on a very high rock, and the spray from the waves was wetting her clothes. Bonnie felt the time was probably right to begin to head back towards the beach.

"Come on, Skye, start coming back this way. I think the tide might be coming in."

"Worryguts," Skye called back, giggling.

"Cheeky monkey!" Bonnie laughed. Skye climbed over a few rocks, and stood looking out to sea. "I can see something over there, Mum." she called. "Is it France?"

"No, probably Wales," Bonnie replied. She turned to look at Dan. He was still skimming stones, every so often shielding his eyes to look out at the horizon. She turned back to the rocks, which were suddenly empty. "Skye!" she called, "where are you?" Silence greeted her, and her heart jolted in her chest. She clambered up the nearest rock, calling Skye's name over and over. There was no sign of her daughter but when she looked down, she saw Skye's cap floating in the water.

"Dan, Dan!" she screamed. She threw herself into the water. Skye must have slipped off the rocks while she was looking the other way. Bonnie flew into the spray, unmindful of the sharp rocks. She put her head under the water, looking for Skye. Where was she? Suddenly Dan was by her side in the water, shouting, asking questions.

"I don't know! I don't know!" Bonnie cried, "she was there, then she wasn't!" They both flung themselves back and forth in the water, soaked now to the skin, desperately searching for some sign of Skye. Dan climbed back onto the rocks and looked around. There must be some sign of his daughter, she couldn't just disappear. It wasn't feasible.

By now a small crowd had gathered, wondering at the commotion. "Shall I call the coastguard?" a woman with a dog asked.

"Oh yes, oh yes please!" Bonnie gasped, before diving back into the surf. She was sure Skye must be somewhere nearby. Her legs had turned to jelly, and her stomach was shaky and sick. She floundered around, stumbling over rocks, cutting her legs and hands. Suddenly a hand seized her arm, and she was unceremoniously pulled out of the water. A coastguard supported her as she stood on the beach, shaking and shivering.

Bonnie collapsed heavily onto the sand. A blanket appeared around her shoulders, and a cup of tea was placed in her hand. She watched the coastguards. She saw the lifeboat come into view. She saw the police and ambulancemen arrive. Skye did not reappear.

TWO

A policeman sat down next to Bonnie.

"Mrs Taylor, it's dark now, we need to call off the search until morning." Bonnie looked up aghast, at the tall, young policeman. He was taller than Dan, probably over six foot, and he looked no older than twenty, although she supposed he must be older than that.

"You can't give up, my baby's in the water somewhere!" she cried.

"I know, and I'm sorry" he said, "but we can't do anything in the dark. We'll get police divers out at first light. I suggest you go back to your house and try and get some rest."

"Mum! Oh, Mum!" Bonnie heard, and she turned around to see Summer flying up the beach towards her, hair streaming around her head as she ran. Dan was not far behind, his long legs pumping. "Oh, Mum, what happened?" Summer asked, throwing herself into Bonnie's arms. Bonnie put her arms around Summer, hugging her tightly. She was unable to speak, suddenly overwhelmed at the realisation that she could hold Summer, but not Skye. A moan escaped her. Summer held her tighter, and the two of them sat on the beach in the gathering twilight, sobbing as if they would never stop. Dan sat down beside them, and put his arms around the pair of them, his tears mixing with theirs.

A policewoman joined them at some stage, waiting until this initial burst of grief had passed. When Dan pulled away to wipe his eyes, she inclined her head at him. "Mr Taylor, my name's Wendy Usher, and I'm assigned to be your family liaison officer. Can I help you to get back to your cottage? It's getting late and cold, and I think your wife needs to get warm." It was true that Bonnie had begun to shiver uncontrollably, although this was more likely due to shock than cold.

Wendy walked back to Rose Cottage with them. "I'll come inside with you for a while," she said as they reached the empty cottage. She was slightly older than Bonnie, probably in her early forties, taller than average, slightly plump. Her faded brown hair was pulled back in a loose pony tail. While the kettle was warming, she went upstairs and started the bath running. All the while Bonnie stood in the middle of the kitchen, the blanket around her shoulders, a blank look in her eyes. Dan sat at the table, his head in his hands, and Summer paced between them, chewing on the ends of her hair. Wendy poured them all mugs of tea, and told Bonnie that she had run her a bath. "I don't want to," Bonnie said listlessly.

"No, but you need to warm up," Wendy replied, and gently led her up to the bathroom.

Bonnie sat in the bath, hugging her knees. She couldn't stop shaking and her mind was stuck on a continual loop where she could see Skye on the rocks, and then not there. She shouldn't have turned away! She should have turned back a few moments sooner! Had she heard some tiny sound from Skye? Why hadn't she been more careful? Why hadn't she listened to Dan? What could she do to get Skye back? Could Skye survive in the water until the morning? She wasn't a strong swimmer. Tears ran down her face, falling off her chin to land in the rapidly cooling water.

Back down in the kitchen, there was a smell of cooking. Dan and Summer sat at the round wooden table, looking lost. They both reached out to Bonnie as she came down the stairs in her blue nightdress and a green cardigan. She wore a pair of Dan's thick woollen socks on her feet in place of slippers. She sat down, and soon found a plate of food placed in front of her. She felt horribly full, as if she would never be able to eat again. Looking up at Dan, she tried to speak, wanting to explain that it was not possible for her to swallow food right now, but she found him looking back at her, his face mirroring her own stricken expression. Bonnie put her fork back down on the table, and drank her cup of tea. She watched Summer spiritlessly pushing her potatoes around on her plate.

"Summer, you don't have to eat it if you don't want to," she said. Summer nodded, and put her hands in her lap.

None of them were able to find the right words to say to each other. From time to time Bonnie and Dan asked each other unanswerable questions; "Is she going to be OK?" "Do you think she's still alive?" Whatever they said sounded trite and meaningless, and by nine o'clock they had more or less given up speaking. Wendy offered to stay all night with them, but there was no reason to take her up on her offer. Their main worry was that there was no way for the police to contact them quickly if anything happened. There was no telephone in the cottage. Bonnie, Dan and

Summer all had mobile phones with them, but Lynmouth was set in such a deep valley that they were unable to get a signal.

"I promise I shall come back immediately we have any news," Wendy said as she prepared to leave them. "Otherwise, I'll come back in the morning. Are you sure you don't want me to stay?"

Bonnie and Dan nodded, and then watched as Wendy walked through the dark to her car, which was parked by the river wall.

Summer stood in the doorway of the sitting room, her mouth set in a firm line, her hands clasped into fists by her side, a noticeable tremor in her arms. Bonnie sat her on the sofa and sat beside her, tightly holding her hand. Dan turned the television on, the sound down low. An audience was laughing along with a comedian, and the sound of their mirth turned Bonnie's stomach. She looked over at Dan to see if he was laughing, but he was staring straight through the screen, tears coursing down his cheeks.

Summer had slumped to one side on the sofa, her swollen eyelids drooping. Bonnie moved a cushion under her head, straightened her legs out and covered her with the car blanket which had been left in a heap by the door. Summer murmured and tried to sit up, but Bonnie shushed her and stroked her hair until she quietened.

She walked into the kitchen and filled the kettle. Searching through the cupboards, she found the teabags and cups. She moved around the kitchen, tidying plates and food boxes as she went. Under the sink she found a cloth and some washing up liquid, and with these proceeded to clean the sink and work surfaces. Once the kettle had boiled, she made two cups of tea and carried one in to Dan. She placed it by his side, touching his shoulder before returning to the kitchen.

Bonnie sat at the kitchen table with her drink. The tea was hot and its warmth comforted her a little. She drank the tea slowly, staring sightlessly out of the window. Once her cup was empty, she stood up and refilled the kettle, taking another teabag out of the box. While the kettle heated up again she sat back down at the table, her chin resting on her hand. Her head sagged heavily.

"Mummy! Mummy! I want to come home!"

Bonnie lurched upwards in her seat, fully awake, her heart pounding, her breath caught in her throat. "Skye?" she called. Dan appeared in the doorway, his eyes wide, the pupils huge and dark. "What is it?" he asked.

"Dan, I heard Skye's voice, as if she was right here! She called me and said she wants to come home. Oh, Dan, where is she? What does it mean?"

"Oh, Bonnie. It's only natural that you'd think you heard her."

He sat down next to her, but Bonnie was unable to rest. She stood up and walked into the sitting room. Summer was asleep, sprawled across the sofa, her face blotched and puffy from the tears she had shed during the evening. Bonnie sat in the chair nearest to the window and sat staring out into the night.

What had happened to Skye? If she had fallen into the sea, why had there been no trace of her seconds later? But what else could have happened? Bonnie had an urge to do something, to somehow find Skye and make things better. She stood and paced the room, sobs jerking her body from time to time.

"Mummy! Please help me!"

Bonnie jolted as if electrocuted. The hairs on her arms stood upright, and her scalp prickled. That had been no dream, she was wide awake. But it was definitely Skye's voice; she could hear the slight lisp which she had never managed to get rid of. Oh God! Was she going mad? Where *was* Skye? She ran to the front door, tugging it open and rushed out into the lane. "Skye! Skye!!" She called, "where are you?" She heard windows being flung open behind her, and saw Dan coming out of the house, but she didn't hear Skye. She only heard the sound of her own blood pulsing through her head, and the breath whistling in and out of her constricted throat.

***

Mary Hawkins led a simple life these days. Since Paddy had passed away four years earlier, she lived alone in her small, cluttered cottage. She didn't eat much, and she kept herself to herself. Liked to watch a bit of television (but none of that mucky stuff they put on later at night), and she read romantic novels from the library. She had a few friends - Jenny Smith from number 12, and Gladys Walker from round the corner. They met for tea in each other's houses, and went to bingo together twice a week, but otherwise Mary was content to be left alone.

She stood at the kitchen sink, washing her breakfast bowl and teacup. She worked slowly, dreamily moving the suds around with her rubber-gloved hands. There was nowhere she needed to go today, she was in no hurry. She gazed out of the window as she worked. That Mr

Ballard next door was a lazy beggar. His lawn could do with cutting; it must be nearly two feet high now. He was an unsociable so-and-so too, barely had the manners to say good morning to her. Good manners cost you nothing, Mary liked to say, but he was too mean to be polite. She leaned forwards, her attention caught by something out of the corner of her eye. What was different about his house today? Why, it looked as if he had nailed hardboard over the inside of his cellar windows! How peculiar! Whatever could he be up to in there? Probably distilling illegal whiskey or something of the kind. He looked the type to drink too much. Humph.

Mary turned away, pulling the rubber gloves off her arthritic hands. The warm water had eased the pains in her joints a bit, that was good. It was 9.30. She might as well go to the shops now. Maybe she would meet Gladys on the way. They could have a laugh together about how odd Mr Ballard was.

She put her coat on, picked up her handbag, and walked out into the sunny morning.

THREE

Wendy Usher arrived at the cottage later that morning. Bonnie had not slept at all, and she felt wrung out, but edgy and restless. Dan had retreated into his shell, and was hardly speaking to anybody. He seemed to have aged ten years overnight. Summer, on the other hand, looked like a lost child, tears constantly filled her eyes, and she carried Skye's toy dog around with her, hugging it like a security blanket. Her dark wavy hair was unbrushed, the curls standing out from her head like cotton wool.

"The police divers went out at first light," Wendy said. "They'll let you know as soon as they find anything. I think I ought to warn you that the press have arrived at the beach. Please don't be upset, Bonnie, but they received a tip-off that a young girl had been lost in the sea, and they are filming the divers. If you go down to the beach, you might bump into them. It might be best for you to stay here today." Her grey eyes were creased with concern, her forehead wrinkled with worry.

Bonnie's eyes filled with yet more tears. She wanted to go to the beach, sure she would be able to find some clue there as to what had happened to Skye. She didn't want to sit here with nothing to do, feeling so helpless.

"I must do something!" she pleaded. "I can't just sit here! What can I do?" Wendy shook her head.

"It's up to you, Bonnie, you can go out if you want, but you need to be prepared for the press. They might ask you all sorts of questions, and you need to be ready for that."

"Well, I'm going!" Bonnie said, and rushed upstairs to throw some clothes on. She stood in front of the wardrobe, unable to make the simple decision about what to wear. She grabbed at a pair of jeans and a T-shirt. Looking at her reflection in the mirror, she hardly recognised the unkempt woman before her. At just over five feet tall she would never look slim and willowy, but this morning she looked lumpen. She smoothed the T-shirt down over her stomach, and ran an afro comb through her thick, curly hair. The least she could do for Skye was to allow her the dignity of not having a mad-looking mother in the newspapers. She considered putting on some lipstick, but felt it was a frivolous gesture, unsuitable for today.

When she came back down, everybody was waiting at the bottom of the stairs, looking up at her. She held her hand out to Summer. "Come on, love, comb your hair and we'll go out." She searched until she found some dark glasses for herself and Summer. Dan watched her from his seat at the kitchen table. "Do you want to come with us Dan?" she asked.

He shook his head. "I can't, Bonnie, I just can't," he said despairingly. Bonnie nodded. She reached out her hand to stroke his hair, but hesitated, her hand an inch away from his head, before dropping her arm back down to her side. She reached out instead and took Summer's hand, and they went to the front doorway. She pulled open the heavy door, pausing on the step before putting her foot into the outside world.

The sun was shining, and tourists were walking along by the side of the river, laughing and talking to each other. Boys fished off a big rock. It looked as though the world was going on as normal, as if nothing had happened. It wasn't right that the world should just keep turning like this - how dare all these people have a good time when Skye was missing? Bonnie rushed down towards the seafront, blinded by tears, sobs catching in her throat. She stumbled as she reached the bridge, and would have fallen if it were not for Wendy gripping her arm and leading her towards the beach, where there were crowds of photographers and onlookers. "Bonnie," Wendy said quietly, her plump cheeks pink from the exertion of running after Bonnie, "it would be useful if we had a photo of Skye we could release to the press. It would keep them away from you a bit."

Bonnie looked at her. "I'm on holiday with my family!" She almost spat, "Why would I have a photo with me? I thought I would be able to see Skye whenever I wanted!" Her voice caught on the last words, snarled up with the emotions she was barely able to keep in check.

"What about somebody at home?" Wendy persisted, "Is there anybody who would have access to a recent picture of Skye?"

"Yes, my mother can get you a picture," Bonnie said, defeated. She gave Wendy her mother's name and address, looking around, trying to ignore all the people near her. She wanted to get back to the rocks where she had last seen Skye.

"Shall we go over to the rocks?" she asked, but Summer shook her head.

"I'd rather stay on the beach; I'll sit here and wait for you."

Bonnie was troubled. She wanted to climb the rocks, and see if she could remember exactly where she had last seen Skye, but she was terrified of letting Summer out of her sight for even a moment. Supposing she disappeared too?

Wendy seemed to read the dilemma on her face, as she said;

"Summer could stay with me, Bonnie. I'll keep an eye on her until you come back." Bonnie thought about it for a moment, then thanked Wendy and moved towards the shoreline.

Disregarding the warnings from the police, Bonnie climbed up onto the rock where Skye had last been seen. She looked around her, turning 360 degrees, gazing from the water to the sky, to the cliffs behind her. She noticed that she was really not all that far from the cliffs. It was odd that Skye had fallen into the water from here - it would have seemed more likely that she would have fallen onto a rock. Oh, if only she had! She may have been hurt, but at least she would be here with her now! Bonnie clambered down towards the cliffs. Just behind her was a small cave. She had been unable to see it from the beach, and would not have noticed it if she hadn't climbed down the cliff side of the rocks. She moved into the opening. Although it was invisible from the beach, from the mouth of the cave she could look out onto the rocks. She could see the police and some of the onlookers, and observe the boats out on the sea. Bonnie looked around her at the little cave. It was narrow, and went back a few feet into darkness. The sea must wash into here at high tide. It was damp and smelled salty and dank. She wished it was possible to stay here; it felt the closest she was likely to get to Skye again in the near future. She sat down on the wet sand, overwhelmed by despair. Alone, she felt able to let the tears overpower her, weeping painfully, the sobs dragged out of the very core of her being.

Some time later Bonnie heard a call; "Mum? Where are you?" and Summer's worried face appeared at the mouth of the cave. "Mum?" she asked. Bonnie tried to smile, and held her hand out to Summer. She stood up; her legs numb from sitting on the damp sand, and started towards her daughter. As she turned, something in the corner of the cave caught her attention. She moved towards it, wondering what was glimmering in the dimness. She bent down, her hand moving out towards the small item, and suddenly swayed, almost blacking out, a small "ohhh" escaping her. She put her fingers out, and brought the object back towards her face, unable to believe what she was seeing.

"Mum? What is it, Mum?" Summer called.

Bonnie turned towards her, her hand held out in front of her. "Oh, Summer!" she whispered, "Look! It's Skye's necklace! The one Nana gave her for her birthday!" She passed the silver ornament to Summer, who turned it over wonderingly. It was a silver dolphin, with a ruby for an eye, an unusual piece of jewellery, which Skye loved. Mother and daughter looked at each other, then hastened out of the cave towards Wendy.

Bonnie and Summer rushed towards Wendy, who was talking to two policemen a few yards away from the rocks.

Bonnie held out her trembling hand, the necklace dangling from her fingers.

"Look what I found!" she exclaimed. "It's Skye's necklace. I found it in a little cave behind the rocks where I last saw Skye. She must have been in the cave and lost it somehow. Look!"

Wendy gently plucked the necklace from Bonnie and handed it to the taller of the policemen. He took it from her, turning it over in his hands before asking; "Are you absolutely sure it is your daughter's necklace?"

"Yes!" Bonnie said, "Yes! It's quite unusual. I don't think I've ever seen anyone else with one. Skye wore it all the time. What do you think?"

The policeman had taken Skye's necklace, but he did not appear to be terribly interested in the discovery. "It may have fallen from her neck while she was playing on the rocks, and been washed into the cave by the tide." he said. *Bastard!* Bonnie thought. Why wasn't he excited by the discovery of such an important clue? He simply passed the necklace to a colleague, who bagged it up and put it in a case.

Bonnie sat down on the sand. She felt drained. She watched the divers coming and going in the water, idly letting sand flow between her fingers. She looked at her watch, but it was only just after ten. This day was going to last forever, she felt. She looked back at the rocks, remembering again and again the last time she had seen Skye there. How long had she looked away for? Was it ten seconds? Twenty? Why had she turned to look at Dan just then? And had she, just out of the corner of her eye, seen something happening as she turned back? If she could only live through yesterday once more, she would never turn away from Skye, not for a moment. Her eyes felt scratchy and sore from crying, and the sun glinting harshly off the green sea wasn't helping. With a sigh she turned back toward Summer, who lay on her stomach on the sand next to her, her chin on her fists, her eyes glazed over. Bonnie reached out and pushed some hair away from Summer's face. Summer looked at her and tried to smile, although her mouth didn't seem to recognise the impulse. She leaned over towards Bonnie and lay her head in her lap. They sat like that on the sand and watched as the tide went out and then came in again.

***

In the cottage, Dan sat and gazed out at the surging river, a cold cup of tea by his elbow. He wished he had gone to the beach with Bonnie and Summer, but felt unable to face the scene. He had been incapable of telling Bonnie of the guilt he felt at not having saved his daughter. It was all his fault. He knew that the tides were dangerous, but he had done nothing to stop Skye from playing on the rocks, other than ineffectually telling her to be careful. And to just go off down the beach and skim stones was bordering on neglect. He was supposed to be the head of the household, and just look where he had got them! He knew that any moment now Bonnie would realise his culpability, and would lose all respect for him. He put his head in his hands and cried, harsh tears he was unused to shedding, making him gulp and gag.

***

The police and divers continued their search of the beach and water, but came up with no further clues. Later

31

in the afternoon, Bonnie found herself sitting a few yards from two policemen, who were discussing the fact that they were consulting experts to find out where a body would be likely to be washed up from here. "That way, we know which forces to contact to keep a look out for us, so that they can get to the body before any passers-by find it," the elder of the two men finished, his face pink and shiny with sweat. Bonnie leapt to her feet, anger coursing through her veins. A body! Skye was not a body. Even if she was dead she would never be a body to Bonnie. She would always be her baby, her youngest daughter. Oh, how she wanted her back! The pain was deep inside her, coupled with a feeling of panic, of wanting to rush out and find Skye. She categorically couldn't accept that Skye was dead. Surely a mother would know if her child was dead? She would just ....

"Mummy! Help me Mummy!"

Bonnie shot up from the ground. "Did you hear that?" she asked, "Wendy?"

Wendy looked mystified. "What, Bonnie? I didn't hear anything," she said.

"It was Skye! She called me! You must have heard! Summer? Didn't you hear her?"

Summer shook her head. She was staring at the ground, focusing on a stone at her feet. Wendy was looking at Bonnie, an air of concern on her face. "What did you hear, Bonnie?" she asked.

"It was Skye! Surely you must have heard her? She called me, said 'Help me Mummy'. Oh, please tell me you heard it too? She must be somewhere near here!" Bonnie glanced at the faces around her. Wendy, Summer and the police officers were looking troubled, all staring at her. Bonnie felt an icy weight descend on her. Nobody but she could hear Skye! Was she going crazy? She honestly didn't think so. A mother's bond to her child was stronger than anybody else's, that must be why she could hear, when nobody else could. Also, Skye was calling to *her*. But how could Bonnie make them believe her?

Shakily, she turned and faced Wendy. "I know I heard her. I heard her last night, twice, and then again now. You may not believe me, but I know what I heard. My daughter is alive somewhere, and she needs me. What *I* need is for you to believe me and to help find my daughter. Now I'm going back to the cottage, come on, Summer," she said, with as much dignity as she could muster, and began walking back up the beach.

FOUR

Skye sat in the corner, shivering. She looked around her, trying to find something in her surroundings which was ordinary. The floor was hard and cold. It looked and felt like dried mud, and it had a dusty, musty smell. The mattress which she was sitting on was a bit smelly too, and the duvet which covered her smelled like old ladies. It was dark in this room, and Skye didn't like it one bit. At home, if it was dark she would cuddle her toy dog until she stopped being afraid, but this was different. There was no toy dog, no Mummy and Daddy down the hall, no Summer in the next room to call to if she was really afraid. And she was really afraid.

When the man had snatched her off the rocks she had been scared, but somehow it had not felt as bad as this. She had been so surprised when he grabbed her from behind - she had thought that she and Mummy were the only people there on the rocks. She had tried to cry out, but the man had put his hand over her mouth very hard, and pulled her up into a little cave above the rocks. At first she had thought that she would be strong enough to get away from him. She had always been good at sports, and could beat Summer at tug-of-war, but this man was ever so strong. He had pulled and pulled until she was right back in the cave, and then he had pushed her through a really small hole at the back. She didn't think he would fit through, but he had just managed, and had even been able to keep his hand over her mouth the whole time. She did think she had heard Mummy call her name as they went, but she couldn't be sure, with the sound of the waves crashing over the rocks. He had dragged her up smelly, slimy rocks until they were up on the hill, and the man had his car there. He had tied a cloth over her mouth. She hadn't liked that at all, and then he put her in the boot of the car and drove off.

She had thought she would be back with Mummy and Daddy soon, but here she was, ages later, and there was no sign of them yet. The man had said that they wanted him to look after her for a while so that Mummy could have a rest, but that didn't really sound like her to Skye. If Mummy was tired she would rest on the sofa and ask Skye to play quietly - she had never asked anyone to look after her for a few days.

Skye wondered when the man would come back to the room she was in, or had he forgotten about her already? Yesterday he had brought her some food and drink. Funny food. He had brought her little iced cakes, and cola to drink. The kind of food she had at parties. He said they were going to be good friends, but that was silly. He was at least as old as Daddy, and she didn't want to be his friend. Of course, she hadn't told him that, she was too scared of what he might do if she made him angry. She had just nodded and tried to smile, although her face felt puffy from crying, and her nose was blocked with tears. She thought it was probably best if she was a good girl, then the man might let her go home sooner. She thought that was what he had meant last night when he had said;

"Be a good girl now. I won't be able to let you go home if you make too much fuss."

All night long she had been crying and calling to Mummy. She couldn't believe that she had let her go like that. She kept on and on calling her, until the man had come and asked her, quite kindly, to please be quiet. He said that Mummy would get cross if she kept shouting out like that. Skye didn't think so, she knew that Mummy would always help her if she was in trouble, but she had asked, "Is Mummy here then? Can she hear me?" The man had just smiled, and patted her on the head.

"Go to sleep, dear. Mummy is having a rest; she doesn't want to be disturbed." And then he had turned out the light.

Skye wondered what she had done so wrong to make them send her away. Was it because she had laughed at them when Daddy had told them to be careful on the rocks? Or because she had argued with Summer last week and broken her lipstick? She knew she hadn't always been a good girl. She did try to be good, but sometimes she forgot. Mummy had shouted at her a few days ago for following her around all the time and getting under her feet. "I just wanted to be with you, Mummy," she whispered now, "I'm sorry if I was naughty and in the way."

Skye couldn't help crying. She was so scared, and she wanted Mummy and Daddy and Summer so badly. She called to Mummy inside her head; asking to please let her come home, please help her.

Eventually she had cried herself to sleep, hugging the edge of the duvet to her as if it was her toy dog. Her dreams were of home, of sitting in the kitchen with her family surrounding her, with Daddy reading the paper while Mummy said, "Don't read at the table, Dan, you're setting a bad example," and she and Summer laughing at him as he made a face behind Mummy's back. Mummy making boiled eggs and soldiers for breakfast. The sun shone into the kitchen and Skye could smell the toast cooking and Daddy's coffee brewing. She had awoken this morning, shocked to find herself still here in this horrible room, away from her family still. There was light licking around the edges of the boards which covered the windows, and she could hear birds singing outside.

In the end she had had to give in and use the bucket in the corner which was supposed to be her toilet, although she hated to use it, and was afraid the man would come in and see her on it.

Now she sat quietly, wondering what was going to happen to her today. Would the man feed her again? Skye had always liked a big breakfast, often eating two or three bowls of cereal before school, and she was quite hungry now. She listened until she heard his footsteps descending the stairs, and she sat up straighter.

***

Wendy followed Bonnie and Summer along the beach. She caught up with them as they reached the path. "Bonnie, do you want to phone your mother about the photo, or would you rather we contacted her?" she asked.

Bonnie looked at her. Wendy was a very kind, professional woman, but at the moment she almost hated her. "Don't even think about sending the police to my mother! Don't you think she'll be upset enough as it is?" she said, "I'll ring her myself, right now."

Bonnie took her mobile phone out of her pocket. She tried to dial her mother's number, but found that, of course, there was no signal. She searched her pockets for loose change, but found none. She stood on the path, looking down at her hands, unable to decide on a sensible alternative to the mobile phone.

Wendy watched her for a moment, then ventured a suggestion; "Could you perhaps reverse the charges, do you think?" Bonnie nodded, and slowly began walking towards the public phone box, nodding at Summer to stay outside with Wendy.

When she reached the box Bonnie stopped, trying to gather her thoughts. What on earth could she say to her mother? Skye and Summer had always spent a lot of time with Nana, and her mother loved the girls deeply. She did wonder if her mother had seen the papers today, and if she would already know some of what had happened. "Just do it, just do it," she murmured to herself, and put her hand on the door handle. She pulled on the weighty door, which felt excessively heavy. The air inside the phone box felt heavier than outside, thick and musty, and she wondered if she would be able to breathe well enough to speak on the phone. She picked up the dull, black receiver, listening to the hum of the dial tone. Her fingers fumbled at the buttons as she dialled the operator, and she tried to remember the words she wanted to say.

In the end, the connection was made easily enough, and Bonnie was soon able to hear her mother's soft voice, agreeing to accept the call. When they were connected Bonnie drew a deep breath and tried to say 'Mum?' but all that came out was a huge sob.

"Bonnie?" her mother said, so far away down the line, "Bonnie? Is that you, darling? It's OK, I'm here and I've heard the news. Bonnie?"

And Bonnie stood and sobbed into the telephone, while her mother cried at the other end. She held onto the receiver as if to a lifeline, wanting her mother more than she ever had since she was a child.

***

Afternoon light turned to purple dusk. Bonnie and Dan barely spoke, unable to find any words to comfort each other. Bonnie looked ahead to the night with a sense of dread, not wanting to face the sleepless hours before dawn. Dan was sitting wordlessly at the kitchen table, moving a pen back and forth over the tablecloth. At midnight he stood up. "Shall we try to get some sleep?" he asked quietly. They filed up the narrow stairs to the small bedroom under the eaves. Bonnie undressed quickly in the dark, and sank into bed beside Dan. He felt for her hand, and they lay in the dark, hands clasped together like small children afraid of the night.

"Mummy! Mummy! Please Mummy, please Mummy, Mummy!"

Again, Bonnie flew awake, her heart racing. Oh, Skye! She thought. Where are you? How can I help you if I don't know where to look? She lay in the bed, tears coursing down her face and pooling around her ears. Dan reached out and pulled her towards him, holding her as she sobbed incoherently against his shoulder. She had tried to tell him how she could hear Skye calling her, but was conscious that he thought it a figment of her overwrought imagination. She had no idea how to go on. She *knew* that

39

Skye was alive; she just had no idea how to reach her, how to help her, and nobody agreed with her. Dan stroked her shoulders, his hands moving slowly down her back, reaching her bottom, and lingering there. Bonnie leapt up out of bed, pulling her night dress around her as if for protection. That he could think of love-making at a time like this!

"What do you think you're doing?" She hissed at him, afraid of waking Summer in the next room.

"I just thought it would be comforting to make love, it might help us to forget all this for a little while," he said. "I just wanted to hold you for a while, that's all."

"I don't want to forget," Bonnie said, "Skye is my daughter, and I will never forget anything about her!"

She spent the rest of the night in the kitchen, with only the teapot and the gentle hum of the refrigerator for company. Why did men and women have to be so different? she wondered, not for the first time. When she first met Dan she had thought that he was different to the other men she had been out with. She had been working at the same bank where she had been employed since the age of eighteen, and by 1985 she had been working there for six years, and was feeling a little restless. The long grey days in the bank never seemed to end.

One Friday morning a tall young man had come into the bank, asking to open a new account. Bonnie invited him to sit down, and took his details. As he filled in his application form, she surreptitiously looked him over. His hair was dark and curled over his ears, and his brown eyes crinkled at the corners when he smiled, which was often. She noticed that he had a tan, which he couldn't have come by in England this year. He looked up suddenly and grinned as Bonnie blushed. He leaned towards her, and read the name on her badge. "Bonita Scott. Nice to meet you, Bonita," he said, and held out his hand. Bonnie looked down at the form on the desk, shook his hand, and said, "Pleased to meet you too, Daniel Taylor."

"Dan," he said.

"Bonnie," she countered. They were both laughing by this time.

"Are new customers allowed to ask bank staff to have a drink with them?" Dan asked.

"I guess it would be OK, as long as you're not trying to sweet-talk me into giving you an overdraft," Bonnie replied, feeling proud of her wit. Dan had smiled, and asked her to meet him that evening. Bonnie had intended to go to the local pub with her best friend, Cath, but decided Cath would understand. After all, you couldn't turn down an opportunity like this!

Dan took her out for a pizza that evening, followed by a few drinks in the pub. Bonnie did not let on that he was the first man ever to invite her out to dinner, but she was charmed. In the restaurant, her mouth was so dry that she was afraid she would be unable to swallow pizza. Looking at the menu she tried to decide what would be the least embarrassing thing to order. She loved spaghetti, but would probably end up splattering sauce all over her face and clothes if she ordered that. Lasagne was another favourite, but she often found that it was too hot and burned her mouth. She didn't think Dan would find her very alluring if she sat fanning her open mouth with her hands.

Salad was an option, but she didn't want to be munching loudly on crispy leaves.

She looked up to find Dan looking at her over the menu, a smile on his face. "Decided yet?" he asked.

Bonnie shook her head. "It all looks so good," she said to buy time, "what are you having?"

"Pizza," he replied, "With salami and cheese. My favourite. What do you like?"

"Everything!" Bonnie answered, then blushed, thinking he would think she was a pig. "Umm, I think I'll have a pizza too then. Same as yours."

They had a lot to talk about. Dan was working as a trainee solicitor, which Bonnie thought must be very interesting. She asked him about his job, and he made her laugh, describing some of the characters who came into his offices.

"You must get some weirdos in the bank too?" he asked.

She grinned. "Oh yes, especially the young ones who try and chat me up!" And they had laughed at that. Dan edged his hand across the table until it touched Bonnie's. He looked into her eyes as he pulled her hand into his. He lifted her hand to his lips, blushing slightly as if aware that it was a corny gesture, but Bonnie's heart fluttered and she felt a stirring somewhere below her stomach.

Before the evening was over, she knew that she wanted to see Dan again. If it hadn't been such a silly thing to think, she would have thought she was in love with him already. Of course, she was far too sensible and down to earth to believe in love at first sight.

Bonnie stood up from the kitchen table and put her mug in the sink. Perhaps she had been a bit hard on Dan. She knew that he loved her, and had often considered herself lucky that he still desired her after nearly fifteen years of marriage. She made her way quietly back up the stairs, feeling her way in the dark. As she approached their bedroom she became aware of a noise, and as she drew nearer she realised that it was the sound of sobbing. Hesitating outside the door, she listened for a moment to Dan's smothered crying, her hand hovering above the door handle, before turning away and tiptoeing back to the kitchen.

The next morning, Wendy again arrived at the cottage early. She sat them down in the kitchen to explain that the police needed to search the cottage - and their home in Essex. "It's routine when children go missing," she said, "I'm sorry." Horrified, Bonnie and Dan watched the team of police arrive to begin the search. They moved quietly through the cottage, picking up every item, turning things over, opening and examining every pot and box. Without exception all drawers were opened, each item of furniture was lifted off the ground and looked under.

Bonnie felt bile rise in her throat. Presumably she and Dan were under suspicion to some extent. She felt sorry for her mother, at their house in Westcliff, presumably going through the same thing. Oh, she hoped her mother did not think that she had done something to Skye! Did all this mean that the police had found something? Did they really think Skye was dead? Something terrible had happened to her - was still happening to her - which was why she kept calling for her mother. If only she could find some way of making everybody else understand! But whenever she tried to talk about it, she saw the same blank, embarrassed look come over their faces, the way they nodded over politely at what she had to say.

Earlier this morning Bonnie had seen two young children running past the cottage, lunchboxes in their hands, and had been sharply reminded of the day Skye had started school. Skye had been very much her baby, and had wanted to stay at home with Mummy all the time. She had been quite excited about starting school however, looking forward to going to big girls' school with her sister. But she had reckoned without the reality of having to say goodbye to Mummy and being left at the school. Bonnie had had to walk away from her, knowing that Skye was tearfully watching her through the big window in the classroom, her teacher standing behind her and trying to entice her to join in with the other children. Halfway home Bonnie had very clearly heard Skye's voice inside her head; *Mummy! Come back! I want to come home with you!* And when she had picked Skye up that afternoon she had asked why she didn't come back sooner, saying; "I called you, Mummy. Mrs Wright said I shouldn't cry any more, so I called and called you inside my head. Did you hear me?" And Bonnie had said that, yes, she did think she had heard her, but now she was a big girl and had to stay at school, but she had been puzzled by it for a long time.

Now Bonnie abruptly stood up from the kitchen table. "I'm going out," she said. She walked down towards the beach, shading her eyes to see how many police were still at the site. Fewer than yesterday, she was sure of that.

That morning she had heard that the police were scaling down their search, and she was furious about it.

As she drew level with the beach, Bonnie veered off to her right, and began to climb up the hill. Where would be a good place to begin searching for Skye? She wondered. She walked up and up, her breath laboured now, a faint sheen of sweat breaking out on her body. At the top of the hill she came to some grassland, and she sat there for a rest. She could see across the bay from here, the steep hill rising up to Lynton, the cliff lift a faint groove on the left side of the precipice.

Bonnie tried to clear her mind. If she was able to hear Skye so clearly, it must be due to Skye calling to her very forcefully. So, all that was needed was for her to do the same, and call powerfully to Skye. She closed her eyes, and focused her mind on her beautiful daughter. She could conjure up Skye's sharp little face, her blue eyes and dark blonde hair. She could even envisage Skye's cheeky smile. Trying not to break down, Bonnie began to call out, silently; "Skye, Skye! Mummy's here! Can you hear me?" She waited, keeping as still as possible, trying to concentrate on her image of her daughter. "Skye! Skye! Please can you hear me? I'm trying to find you! Skye!" The silence pressed down around her, emphasising her aloneness.

Skye was the type of child who was always happy to be with her mother. Although she had many friends, she was still content to be at home or out shopping with Bonnie. They had good times together, cooking or shopping, or playing the everlasting board games which Skye loved. Scrabble was her current favourite, even though she tended to cheat when she had difficult letters.

She and Bonnie would laugh as Skye spelt out made-up words, insisting that they were real. "Tonky isn't a real word!" Bonnie would insist, but Skye would answer; "It must be, or I wouldn't have been able to spell it!"

Bonnie was feeling a physical loss, missing the sense of her youngest child by her side. It was true that she sometimes got cross with Skye, and only last week she had snapped at her for being under her feet all the time. They had been in the kitchen, Bonnie trying to make cakes for the school's summer fete, and Skye had been following her so closely that Bonnie had tripped on her way to the oven.

"Will you get out from under my feet?" she had barked. Oh, that had been so unkind, she now realised. If only she had recognised how lucky she had been to have Skye near her. Was this some kind of punishment for that? No, surely God would not punish her for a normal bad-tempered reaction. Would He?

Bonnie could remember the night Skye was born as if it was yesterday. When she had given birth to Summer three years earlier she had had a long, painful labour, but with Skye things had been much easier. Bonnie had wondered if her body had got used to the idea of giving birth. Her waters had broken at 11 p.m., and Dan had phoned Bonnie's mother to ask her to come and look after Summer. They had been excited as they got ready to go to the hospital. Bonnie's mother had arrived out of breath and with her hair in curlers, which had made them laugh. "Go on you two," she had said, shooing them out the door. Bonnie however had needed to go and take one last look at Summer, sleeping peacefully in her little bed. "It's the last time she'll ever be an only child," she had whispered to her mother, as she stood drinking in the sight of her sweet daughter.

Bonnie now realised with a mounting sense of horror, that Summer might have to get used to being an only child once again.

"Oh, Skye!" she again called, "Where are you, darling? I really, really want to find you!" But Skye didn't answer. The gulls swooped and soared overhead, their shrieks alarming and dreadful in the quiet afternoon air.

FIVE

It was Gladys's birthday, and she had been invited to have dinner with Mary. She arrived at Mary's cottage at 5.30, a bunch of carnations in her hand. Mary opened the door, a big smile on her face. "Happy birthday, Glad!" she said, and hugged her friend.

Mary offered her a sherry while she finished cooking the dinner. "Oh, go on then," Gladys smiled, "just a small one." Mary poured two large sherries, and the ladies stood in the kitchen, sipping their drinks and discussing the neighbours. Gladys updated Mary on the comings and goings of her son, Jim, and how he had bought her a beautiful vase as a birthday present. When they found that their glasses were empty they refilled them, as dinner was not quite ready. Mary cooked as they chatted, putting the finishing touches to the roast dinner which she was cooking as a special treat for her friend.

They ate their dinner at the small table overlooking Mary's tidy garden, drinking a couple of glasses of wine with the meal and gossiping about friends. Mary was reminded of the recalcitrant Mr Ballard.

"Did I tell you about my strange neighbour, Glad?" she asked. Gladys shook her head, so Mary regaled her with the tale of Mr Ballard's boarded-up windows and overgrown grass.

"What do you think he could be up to in there?" Gladys asked.

"Well, I don't know, but I think he could be making illegal whisky or something. He looks the type. Never goes out in the day much, so I think he's probably hung over."

Gladys laughed. "Mary, you do have a vivid imagination!"

"Right, let's go and look!" Mary said, and headed towards the back door.

"What are you doing?"

"I'm going to look over the fence, see what I can see," Mary tiptoed over to the dividing fence, and bent down to peer through a knot hole in the wood. "Can't see anything, Glad," she said in a stage whisper. She looked around her, and then crept towards the apple tree at the side of the house. On her way she seized hold of a garden chair, and dragged it with her. When she reached the tree she climbed carefully on to the chair, and then began to climb into the tree, hitching her flowered dress up over her plump knees as she went.

"Oh, Mary! Do be careful!" Gladys called, her hands flying to her mouth to stifle her giggles.

Mary looked towards Gladys, and put her finger to her lips, then climbed onto the lowest branch of the tree, and edged her way along the bough. She peered over into her neighbour's garden for a while, looking this way and that, before gingerly making her way back to the garden chair. Her permed, grey hair was by now flying out around her pretty pink face, and she had a green smudge on one cheek. Her serviceable brown support stockings were both torn at the knee.

By this time, Gladys was doubled up with laughter. Mary looked at her as she stepped down onto the lawn, smoothing her dress down over her hips. "And what are you laughing at, Mrs Walker?" she asked, trying to hide her own smile.

"Oh, Mary! At your age! You looked as if you thought you were one of the Famous Five!" and Gladys again went off into peals of laughter.

"Hoh, yes!" said Mary, "Just call me George! Hai don't want to be a girl!" and the two women collapsed onto the wooden bench at the back of the house, overcome with mirth.

"My Jim used to love the Famous Five books," Gladys said, wiping her eyes with the sleeve of her blue cardigan, "he always wanted to be Julian. Oh, we used to read those books together all the time."

Mary was by now speechless with laughter. Jim, thinking he could be Julian! Oh dear! Jim had always been a slow, pudgy sort of child, who was shunned by the other children, and he had never had an ounce of adventure in him. He hadn't improved with age either. He was forty-eight now, and had never married. He had never had any obvious friends either, even as an adult. He had started work in the local post office at the age of sixteen, and was still there now. He lived with Glad until the age of forty, and only moved out then because the bungalow next door had been up for sale. Oh dear, oh dear! Of course, Glad thought her only son was a marvel, and had never understood why he was friendless and never had girlfriends.

"You know, Mary, I think we've had a little too much to drink," Gladys said, her face still pink and tear-stained from laughing.

"Oh dear, and I was going to suggest a night-cap!" Mary said.

Gladys laughed. "I'll have a hard enough time getting myself home as it is, Mary!" she said. "If I have any more to drink I'll be incapable".

"Incapable of what, my dear?" Mary asked, waggling her eyebrows at Gladys, which set them both off laughing again.

"No, I really ought to be getting back soon," Gladys said.

"All right, love, I'll make us some coffee before you go. That'll help sober you up a bit," and with that they went back into the cottage.

Next door, Mr Ballard lifted the corner of his kitchen curtain and watched them go.

SIX

Friday morning. Bonnie had not even bothered trying to go to sleep the previous night. There was really no point when she was unable to sleep. She made cups of tea, which she drank as she wandered around the small downstairs of the cottage, always stopping at the front window to look out to the street, as if she might see Skye running up the road towards her. On her return to the kitchen she would switch on the kettle and make yet another cup of tea. This routine was only broken by frequent trips to the bathroom upstairs.

Dan had been up and down to the bedroom, trying to rest but, he too, was not able to sleep. They barely spoke to each other now. Recriminations had been bandied about - why weren't you watching Skye? Why weren't *you?* But they served no purpose.

As the light began to creep round the edges of the curtains, Dan cleared his throat. "We ought to start packing today, Bonnie;"

Bonnie stood and looked at him, her hands on her hips, her mouth drawn into a hard line.

"We have to go home tomorrow;" Dan said, "We've only booked this cottage till tomorrow. There will be other people arriving for their holiday."

"Go home?" Bonnie echoed, "What about Skye?" She was horrified to realise that so much time had passed, and the realisation filled her with misery.

"Bonnie, I don't know what to say;" Dan's forehead was creased into wavy lines, his eyes bleak and weary, "I think we have to accept that there is nothing we can do here. If they were going to find Skye they would have found her by now. If....." he paused, and cleared his throat again, "if they find....... her body, well they'll let us know. We might as well be at home, where Summer can be with her friends, and you can see your Mum."

Bonnie looked at him. She opened her mouth to speak, then shut it again, unable to find any words to use. She sat down at the kitchen table, her head in her hands. The logical part of her brain agreed with Dan, but her heart was telling her that she had to stay here, to be close to Skye.

"What happens when they find Skye alive? What if we're not here?" she asked, her voice barely above a whisper.

"Oh, love! We can come back straight away if they find her;" Dan said, "We could even fly down here if need be. Don't worry about that!" He stood up and came over to where Bonnie sat, and gently placed a hand on her shoulder. Bonnie did not react for a few moments, but then she placed her hand over Dan's. She inclined her head to one side, resting it against his chest, and he put his arms around her. Bonnie let the tears fall, taking some comfort from Dan's nearness. He knelt on the floor, hugging her as tightly as he dared, and Bonnie put her arms around him too, feeling the warm wetness of his tears against her neck.

They were still in this position when Summer came down stairs. "Mum?" she said, "has something happened?"

Bonnie shook her head, and tried to smile. "No, love, but Dad was reminding me that we have to go home tomorrow. We can't stay in the cottage any longer, and I expect you want to see your friends at home."

Summer nodded, and sat at the table.

Leaving Dan and Summer to face the unenviable task of packing, Bonnie announced that she was going out for a walk, and wanted to be alone. She headed towards the nearest bed and breakfast establishment, where she went in and asked if they had any rooms available. Of course, they were all full up - it was the busiest time of the year. She went to every rooming house and hotel in town, even going up in the cliff lift to try her luck in Lynton, but the story was the same wherever she went - there was no room anywhere. She had to concede that it was not going to be possible for her to stay here. There was nowhere to stay, and she could hardly camp on the beach.

Back at the cottage Dan and Summer had begun packing their clothes ready for the trip home. Dan waited until Summer was downstairs before venturing into the girls' bedroom and beginning to fold Skye's clothes. He carefully folded her T-shirts and shorts, delicately placing them into the suitcase. He lifted her toy dog from the bed, holding it as tenderly as if it was made of glass. He headed for the suitcase with it, but got no further than the end of the bed, before stopping, doubled over as if winded. He sat on the edge of Skye's bed, holding the dog to his chest, tears running from his eyes and his breath coming in huge painful gasps. He didn't hear Summer come back into the room, and only became aware of her presence when she knelt before him, her tear-streaked face inches from his. He reached out blindly, gathering his one remaining daughter to him, holding on to her for dear life.

***

Saturday morning came around all too soon. The sun was shining as they loaded their bags into the car, and it looked like the kind of day that they should have begun their holiday with. As Dan made his final preparations before the drive home, Bonnie told him she had something she needed to do before they left. She walked into town, heading for the florist's shop she had noticed the day before. She hovered outside for a while, before deciding. In the shop she bought two dozen roses, and had them wrapped in pink paper. She chose a card with a picture of a teddy, and thought for a while before writing; 'Skye, I miss you more than you will ever know. I will find you soon and bring you back home. I promise. With all my love, always, Mummy.' She walked slowly down to the beach. The tide was out, and there were a few families playing on the pebbly beach. She traipsed across the damp sand until she reached what she now thought of as Skye's rock. Climbing up, she managed to locate the cave where she had found Skye's necklace, and she went inside and placed the flowers in the furthest corner. Kneeling down she said a silent prayer, entreating God to help her find her daughter and bring her safely back home.

Wendy had come along to the cottage to say goodbye. She explained that another family liaison officer would be assigned to them once they arrived home.

Bonnie and Dan thanked her for all her help as they climbed reluctantly into their car. Bonnie was very worried. She knew that Dan and Summer were embarrassed by her protestations that she could hear Skye talking to her, and so she was reluctant to tell them of her concerns, but she wondered if she would still be able to hear Skye back in Essex. Perhaps she could only hear her because she was not too far away. But she had to concede that it was not going to be possible for her to stay here. There was nowhere for her to stay.

As Dan drove slowly up the lane, Bonnie looked back at the beach, feeling as if her heart was being pulled away from her, as though it was trying to stay behind. She kept her eyes focused on the rocks for as long as she was able, only looking away once they were so far up the hill that she could no longer see any part of Lynmouth. She rested her forehead on the cool side window and closed her eyes. For the thousandth time in the past few days, tears leaked from her eyes and ran down her face.

To her surprise, she opened her eyes to find that she had slept for nearly four hours. The exhaustion of the past days had taken its toll, and the movement of the car had lulled her to sleep. She felt dull and bleary-eyed as she turned around to find that Summer was also asleep.

"Are you OK?" she asked Dan, her voice thick with sleep. He nodded, and patted her knee.

"Glad you were able to sleep a bit," he said, "You haven't slept for days."

"It feels like a betrayal to sleep. As if I should be keeping alert or something. I feel as if I've done something wrong by sleeping."

"Oh, Bonnie, you've done nothing wrong!" He looked at her for a moment, and placed his hand on her knee again.

Bonnie managed a small smile for him. The grip on her leg reminded her of their honeymoon. They had travelled by car to Cornwall, and Dan had his hand on her knee almost all the way there. The warmth of his palm had sent electric signals all the way to the top of her thighs, and she had been impatient to reach their holiday cottage. They had stayed for an idyllic week in a cottage not far from Lands End, and it had been a wonderful beginning to their married life. They had planned a day trip to Lands End this holiday, to show the girls where they had stayed. She knew that Skye would have enjoyed standing at the far end of the country, watching the sea whipping the waves into a frenzy.

***

Eventually they reached the outskirts of Westcliff-on-Sea. Bonnie felt her heart racing as the landmarks became more and more familiar. She wanted to get home, but was still dreading it. Her mouth was dry as dust, and her palms were slick with sweat. Looking over at Dan, she was sure that he was feeling the same. His mouth was set in a grim line, and his hands gripped the steering wheel until his knuckles turned white. Every so often he took one hand from the wheel, and rubbed it on his trouser leg. Nobody spoke as they neared their destination. Dan drove up their road slowly, and pulled the car in at the kerb. He turned to Bonnie and opened his mouth as if to speak. He swallowed, and his throat made an audible click. They sat in silence for a moment, looking at each other, neither willing to be the first to make a move.

Suddenly, from the back seat, Summer spoke. "Shall we get out?" her voice was small and worried. Dan nodded, and opened his door. Bonnie climbed out, looking quickly around, hoping that she would not have to see any of the neighbours. From the corner of her eye she noticed the curtains twitch in a window across the road. No doubt Gillian would be over later, but for now she felt able to ignore her.

Dan had by now unlocked the front door, but he was waiting for her to join him. She dragged her way slowly up the short front path, and joined him on the front step. Inside, the house seemed smaller than when they had left it. It smelled familiar, if musty. Bonnie hesitated for just a moment, then cautiously climbed the stairs, and made her way to the small front bedroom where Skye *(had)* slept. She hadn't *really* expected Skye to be there, but even so, she felt her disappointment rising in her as she surveyed the empty room. Skye's favourite yellow duvet cover was on the bed, covered with her beloved soft toys. Bonnie had put her foot down, and only allowed her to take her three most favoured toys on holiday with her; otherwise the car would have been filled with teddies and toy dogs. She sat on the bed and picked up one of the toy dogs, holding it to her face to smell Skye's scent. She felt dizzy. Her heart was thumping, and her breath was coming in short, gasping sobs. She lay down, holding the dog tightly to her chest, holding Skye's aroma tightly in her heart.

SEVEN

"Hello, Bonnie. Can I come in for a moment?" Bonnie's first reaction was to say; "No! Go away and leave me alone!" But of course she didn't. Bill, her church minister, was standing on the doorstep, his concern showing in his face, his eyes damp. She led him into the front room, where he perched on the edge of the sofa, his clasped hands dangling between his knees.

It was Monday morning, and over the past thirty-six hours they had had a number of visitors, all of whom had managed to make Bonnie cry, either by being too kind and concerned, or, like Gillian from across the road, by her fascination at being so close to a newsworthy story. Bonnie's mother had arrived at the house soon after they got home, and they had clung together like lost children, unable to comfort each other. She had stayed over, sleeping on the sofa where Bill now sat, returning home earlier this morning, sad at being unable to help Bonnie through her grief.

"What can I do to help you, Bonnie?" Bill asked now. There was no answer to this kind of question. What could he do? He could go to Lynmouth and find Skye! He could make everybody believe that Skye was really alive, and that she, Bonnie, was as sane as she had ever been! But she couldn't say any of this, so she just shook her head.

"Where is Dan?" Bill asked.

"He's gone to the office. I'm kind of angry with him for going, but at the same time I feel relieved he's not here. We just get on each other's nerves at the moment, tripping over each other wherever we go, and we can't really comfort each other. I feel guilty about it, but I don't really want to talk to him at the moment. I feel as if everything I'm feeling is stuck inside me, and I'm scared that he doesn't understand and we'll end up hurting each other if I say what I really feel." Bonnie paused for breath, and looked up at Bill.

"I guess I needed to get that off my chest," she said. She ought to be ashamed, but she felt the tiniest bit of relief at having spoken.

"I think so," Bill said. "Any chance of a cup of tea, Bonnie? I'm sorry, but I'm really parched."

"Of course," she said, "I've forgotten how to be polite at the moment." She led him out to the kitchen, where he sat at the table while she made a pot of tea. As she worked, Bill talked to her. She was comforted to find that he did not use the trite words and phrases that she was already coming to dread. He admitted there was nothing he could say to comfort her, but wanted to assure her of his love and concern for her and her family.

Sitting in the sun-dappled kitchen, Bonnie felt more at peace than she had all week. Bill was such a good man. He had only been pastor of their church for two years, but she and Dan thought very highly of him. He had come to their church when they had been without a minister for three years, and the congregation were beginning to feel a little unsettled. But Bill had drawn them all together again.

He was able to be friends with all ages, and everybody in the church respected him. Already she knew that they could go to him with any problem, and he would do anything in his power to help or comfort them. He was never judgmental, only ever kind and considerate.

Bonnie turned her cup around in her hands. It was her favourite blue cup, with red poppies growing up the sides. For some reason tea always tasted better out of this cup, and she was the only one who ever used it. Skye had bought it for Bonnie for her last birthday. She swallowed hard over the lump in her throat.

"Bill," she said. He looked up at her, waiting for her to go on. Her heart was racing. She could feel the hot blood pulsing through her veins as she plucked up the courage to say what she needed to say. She looked up at the shelf above Bill's head, her collection of jugs sitting there as it always had, looking for all the world as if nothing in this house had changed. Abandoned on the lower shelf was the horseshoe which Dan had bought so casually on the first day of the holiday. It lay on its side, and Bonnie imagined she could see all the good luck dripping out onto the floor.

"Bill. I don't think Skye's dead." There! She had said it, and Bill was still sitting there, looking at her, not seeming to want to run away.

"Why do you think that?" he asked, eyebrows raised in query rather than surprise, and that opened the floodgates. Bonnie poured her heart out. She told him exactly what had happened the day Skye disappeared, and she told him, haltingly, all about the times Skye had called to her. How she really believed she was hearing Skye, and not some echo from her subconscious. How nobody wanted to believe her, and even her husband and mother thought she was ever so slightly deranged by grief.

Bill sat and took it all in. He did not appear too shocked by what he heard. When Bonnie had finished talking he thought for a moment, his mind in a whirl. He had come here today expecting to give some grief counselling, and now Bonnie had hit him with this. He had only known Dan and Bonnie and their girls for two years, but it was long enough to know that Bonnie was not a hysterical mother. She was generally calm and compassionate with her girls. Very loving, but not obsessive in her affection. It did not seem conceivable that she would imagine something so extraordinary.

"My goodness!" he said at last. "It must be terrible for you, Bonnie."

For one dreadful moment Bonnie thought that he was going to offer her the usual platitudes, a kind of pat on the head for the mad, grief-stricken mother, which she had come to expect over the past days.

"It does sound as if you could have a point; but why are you so sure that what you are hearing really is Skye?" He appeared interested, not disbelieving. Bonnie's heart rate quickened.

Bonnie told him then that she was hearing Skye's voice as she really talked, and went on to explain about the time she had heard Skye calling her on the day she started school. She wiped tears from her face with her sleeve as she talked.

"I wonder what could really have happened to Skye?" Bill asked thoughtfully. "It is weird that they haven't found any sign of her in the water. If she had drowned, I'm sure they would have found something by now. But what do you think could have happened, Bonnie? Where could she be?"

Bonnie felt relief and gratitude wash through her. Bill believed her! He didn't think she was imagining things! She laid her head on her folded arms on the table and sobbed and sobbed. Bill moved round to sit next to her, and put his arm around her shaking shoulders. He said nothing; just let her pour out all her grief.

It was some time before Bonnie was able to lift her head and wipe her face. "I'm sorry, Bill; it is just such a relief to have somebody believe me!"

"No need to apologise," he said, "I find it hard to believe that Dan doesn't understand what is happening."

"Oh, well." Bonnie said, "That's fairly easy to understand. Dan feels guilty, you see. He thinks it's his fault that Skye drowned. He told us to be careful because the tide was coming in, and we didn't take him seriously. He thinks he should have done more to keep Skye safe. Therefore it makes sense to him that she's dead - you know, it's the end of the road because it was all his fault and so therefore there is no point in believing that she is alive."

"I don't believe you could have made this up. What we need to do is think about how we can get people to trust your judgement. It is hard to understand just what is happening here. I believe you, but can understand how others would find it difficult to comprehend." He paused for a moment. "What do the police think?"

Bonnie sighed. "Oh, they think I'm just some mad mother, a bit demented with grief. We had a family liaison officer assigned to us in Lynmouth, and she was replaced by someone here when we got back. John Chambers. He's very pleasant, really supportive and professional. I'm sure that he believes Skye has been washed out to sea. Thinks Dan's the stable one of us. Thinks I need a sedative or something."

Bill nodded. "I suppose you can see their point, Bonnie. They have no evidence that Skye didn't drown. I assume they think that you would want to hear her, and so therefore imagine it. A symptom of your grief."

They sat in silence for a few minutes, each lost in their own thoughts, then Bill spoke:

"When did Skye last call to you?"

"Only this morning, about 10 o'clock. I was cleaning the bath when she spoke. She said; "help me, Mummy," three times. Oh, Bill! How can I help her?"

Bill put his arms around Bonnie's shoulders once more, patting her arm in an effort at comfort.

"I don't know, Bonnie, but I do know that I believe you, if that's any help at all. You can talk to me about this whenever you want, and tell me whenever Skye calls to you if you wish. I can be your friend. It's not much, but it's the best I can do. You must hold on to what you know. You are not going mad, and if I believe you, I'm sure it won't be long till others do too"

He sat and waited patiently as Bonnie cried out her relief, her shoulders shaking under his arm.

EIGHT

Dan tidied up the piles of files on his desk, shuffling them into some kind of order. He picked up a small collection of dictaphone tapes, gathering them together to take to his secretary on his way out. An assortment of pens was collected into a pot on the desk. He looked around, trying to decide if things looked tidy enough to appease the cleaner, who was due in tonight. He swept some notepaper into the top drawer of the desk, and turned towards the door. For the umpteenth time his eyes fell upon the photo on the desk. It had been taken the summer before, during their holiday in Wales. Bonnie, Skye and Summer were sitting on a low wall, squinting into the sun, and laughing at the camera. The girls each held ice creams in their hands, and some had melted, running down the back of Skye's hand. Dan reached out and picked up the picture in its plain brown wooden frame, turning it towards the light, the better to focus on the face of his youngest daughter. He ran his finger lightly over the image of Skye's smiling face, lingering on her upturned chin.

Dan wondered if anybody could really understand the depths of grief of the parents of a drowned or missing child. Everybody he met had been sympathetic, although he noticed that a few of his colleagues were giving him a wide berth. He sympathised with them, as he had often felt at a loss to know what to say to grieving colleagues. A few people he knew had been widowed, but he didn't know anybody else who had lost a child. It was the hardest thing he had ever had to bear, and he often wondered just how he was going to get through the days ahead. He found that he was best if he kept busy. He knew Bonnie resented his being able to go to work, but he didn't know what else to do with himself. He was eaten up with guilt, constantly wishing he could have done more to save his youngest daughter. He could hardly sit at home, day in and day out. He had no idea what to say to Bonnie most of the time, and the more he thought about Skye the worse he felt. Weekends were the worst times; long, empty hours with nothing much to fill them. Before, he would have taken Skye out riding on her bike, or to the shops, but now he felt rudderless and empty. He busied himself as much as possible; tidying the shed, tightening screws on door handles or cutting the grass, but these things could only fill so many hours.

Dan was worried about Bonnie, on top of his own grief and guilt. She could not accept that Skye was dead, and insisted that Skye was calling to her all the time, which was proof in her mind, that Skye was still alive. She hardly ate at all these days, and the weight was falling off her. Often Dan would come home from work to find her still in her nightclothes, her hair unbrushed, and her breakfast still on the table in front of her. He was seriously concerned that she was tipping over the edge into madness, and he was powerless to help her.

Nevertheless he still loved her. He knew that Bonnie was the only woman for him, had known it since the first time he set eyes on her that day in the bank. He had thought her beautiful then, even in the unattractive bank uniform which did not flatter her at all.

If he had had to imagine a situation like this, Dan would have thought that he and Bonnie would pull together, but it didn't bring them closer, anything but. Sometimes he even thought it could herald the end of their marriage. Twice since Skye's disappearance he had tried to make love to Bonnie, and both times it had ended in tears. Bonnie was unable to respond to him in that way and obviously felt offended that he still desired her. Which gave him another reason to feel guilty.

He sighed as he pulled his office door closed behind him. He gave the papers to his secretary, saying goodnight on his way out. His car had been parked in the sun all day, and the air that greeted him when he opened the door was hot, stifling and stale. He stood for a while with the door open to let in some cooler air, before climbing in and starting the engine. The seat was scorching against his back. He leant forward, pulling his hot shirt away from his skin. He wondered why he never remembered to put the sun shade over the windscreen. Although it was September now, the weather had remained hot and sunny for the past weeks, a real Indian summer. He turned on the radio, hoping to find some relaxing music to listen to on the drive.

It was hard to find a parking space when he arrived home, and he had to park some yards away. As he walked towards the house, his stomach was clenched in a tight knot, and his mouth felt dry. He hoped and prayed that Bonnie would be more like her old self today. He fitted his key in the lock, and opened the door. The house was silent, the windows all shut tight as if nobody was home.

"Bonnie," he called into the silence. "Bonnie, are you home?" There was no answer, so he continued into the kitchen, dropping his briefcase on the floor as he went. The kitchen was clean and tidy, with no signs of cooking. He opened the back door to let in some air, and almost fell over Bonnie, who was sitting on the back door step, her face streaked with dirt and tears, a filthy, sun bleached Barbie doll clutched in her hand. Silently Dan sat down next to her and held her to him. She leant against him, almost a dead weight on his chest. A great heaviness of sorrow and grief filled his stomach as he clasped her in his arms.

"Dan," Bonnie said, her voice muffled against his shirt, "tomorrow Summer goes back to school." And with that, understanding flooded through him. Skye should have been going back to school as well, entering her final year of junior school, preparing for her 11+ exam in January, deciding which senior school she would like to go to. He tightened his grip on Bonnie, trying to stop them both from drowning in this sea of despair.

"What have you been doing today?" he asked Bonnie later, when he had managed to manoeuvre her into the kitchen. He was making a cup of tea and some cheese on toast, as it was one of the few things that she managed to choke down these days.

Bonnie shook her head. "I ironed school uniforms," she said. Her mouth was set in a firm line, her eyes downcast. She had ironed Skye's uniform as well as Summer's, in the hopes that Skye would return to wear it. Dan kept his eyes on the grill. He knew, without being told, that Bonnie was preparing for Skye's return to school tomorrow. He had seen the name tapes which she had taken out to sew onto her PE kit. Just in case she turned up in time to return to school. He wondered, briefly, if it would help Bonnie if he shouted at her and became really exasperated. He was trying so hard to be patient and kind. He had heard about tough love, although he was not sure that he was hard enough to go that route. Oh, there were so many situations in life that he was ill-equipped for.

"Where's Summer today?" he asked, returning to a slightly easier subject. Bonnie looked up, thoughts and expressions flitting across her features.

"She went to Sam's house this afternoon. I think she's staying for tea."

Sam was Summer's new boyfriend. They had simply been friends before the tragedy, but since the family returned to Westcliff, Summer and Sam had seen each other almost every day. Dan did wonder about the wisdom of allowing his thirteen year old to spend so much time with her boyfriend, but he had learned that Summer planned to see Sam whatever he said. It was better to allow her the opportunity to be honest with him, rather than forbidding her to see Sam, and putting her in a position where she might be tempted to lie. At least he knew where this daughter was. Summer was acting so differently now. It was as if she felt that she had to mother Bonnie, and she appeared to have matured a great deal over the past few weeks.

He turned the grill off, and turned towards Bonnie with the plates of toasted cheese in his hands. Her head was dipped towards the table, and as Dan watched a single tear dripped off her nose onto the oilcloth.

She looked up at him then, rubbing her hands roughly over her face, and taking a large gulp of air into her lungs. He noticed that her wedding ring slipped around on her finger, looking too big and heavy now.

"I watched television for a while today, Dan," she said. "I watched the film of 'Dr Doolittle' with Eddie Murphy. I thought it might take my mind off things for a while." There was a long pause. "Everybody thought Dr Doolittle was going mad because he said he could talk to the animals - and they could talk to him - but he knew that he really could hear them talk, and they understood him. I feel I'm in the same position – I know I can hear Skye talking to me, but everybody else thinks I'm going mad. Dan, why don't you believe me? Why is this so hard?" The last words were almost unintelligible as her voice broke.

Dan reached across the table for her hands, stroking her palms. "I don't know, Bonnie. I wish I could believe you. I don't want us to fall out or disagree with each other, but I don't hear anything. And if I did, I think it would be too painful to bear. Just the thought of Skye being alive somewhere and us being unable to help her! It's just too much, Bonnie." Now he was crying too, great heaving sobs which shook his shoulders.

Bonnie stood up. Tears still running down her face as she looked at him. "It sounds as if you are just a big coward," she spat the words at him. "You need to grow up and have the courage to find your daughter and bring her home. It's not about you and how you feel."

And with that she left the room, shutting the door so carefully that Dan heard each part of the latch click into place.

NINE

Skye woke up early. The man was moving around upstairs doing something.

"Mummy! Mummy! Please come and get me! I want to come home now!" she called inside her head. "Please, Mummy! I promise I'll be good forever more if you let me come home now!" The man was quite kind to her really, but she still wanted to go home more than anything.

Skye wiped her eyes. It sounded as if the man was washing up. He had asked her to call him 'Buddy', which was a funny name. He said all his friends called him Buddy. He had never been nasty to her. She had been worried about that for a long time at first. At school they had talked about 'stranger danger', and Skye thought that strange men must always do horrible things to you. But not Buddy. He never let her come upstairs during the day, but in the evenings he would take her upstairs into the lounge, where all the curtains were pulled and he liked to play board games. He had Scrabble and Monopoly and a few other games. Skye didn't mind this, as the games took her mind off Mummy and Daddy for a little while. Then he would sometimes let her have a bath, if she promised to be quick and quiet. Whenever they played games, Buddy would bring them crisps and cakes and cola. It was almost like a funny sort of party – with only one friend who you didn't like very much.

Skye still cried every night, and every morning when she woke up and found herself still in the cellar. Each night she dreamed about home, and the dreams seemed to get more real each night. Sometimes the dreams were a bit sad and she would see Mummy and Daddy and Summer crying because Skye wasn't with them. They were horrible dreams, and she really, really cried after those. But she liked to dream about home, because she was scared that she had been here so long that she might forget what home was like, and then Mummy and Daddy and Summer would forget her too, and maybe they would think they had only ever had one girl!

Buddy was coming down the stairs now. Skye could hear the clump, clump of his horrible baggy old slippers. He walked into the room with a tray of food.

"Ta da! Breakfast!" he said, as if he was a magician or something. Skye tried to smile – she knew he liked it if she tried to be brave and happy.

"Thank you, Buddy" she said politely. On the tray was a glass of orange, a bowl of cocoa pops and some toast and jam. She started to eat the cocoa pops, as Buddy stood and watched her.

"I've got a surprise for you today!" he said. Skye looked up warily. Was he going to send her home? Oh, she hoped so!

"I thought for a treat I'd take you out shopping today!" he said. "You really do need some new clothes, and I haven't got anything that would fit you! So I thought we could go for a nice drive to Exeter. You must pretend to be my daughter and call me Daddy. Do you think you could do that?"

Skye nodded. She would be glad to go outside for a little while. Maybe they would meet a policeman while they were out, and he would recognise her and take her home! Mummy and Daddy must have told the police she was missing by now. She had seen pictures in the papers before of children who had gone missing. The policeman would recognise her from the papers, and he'd say to Buddy; "Excuse me, sir, is this really your daughter?" Oh, that would be wonderful!

After Skye had finished her breakfast, Buddy brought her a bowl to wash in, and her T-shirt and jeans, which he had washed. She bathed quickly. She found that her legs were shaking as she pulled her jeans on, and she couldn't seem to do the button up very easily. When she was ready, she sat down to wait for Buddy. He came down the stairs slowly, and before he got to the bottom, he called out and asked if she was decent. Skye had been worried when she was first here, that he might watch her get dressed or washed, but he was very polite and always asked if she was ready. She was glad about that.

Skye walked up the stairs in daylight for the first time. Buddy made her wait in the hall for a little while, and then he came and knelt down in front of her. "I know this is difficult, but I need you to help me," he said. "I don't want anybody round here to see you in the car. They might wonder who you are. They don't know you are my friend. Do you understand?"

Skye nodded, but didn't really understand. She wasn't Buddy's friend! She didn't want to be his friend, even if he was kind and polite, but she didn't dare say so. She knew what could happen to children who were taken by strange men, and had been surprised that Buddy was treating her so well. She didn't dare to upset him in case he changed into the monster she was so afraid he might really be.

"Right," he said then, "I will take you through this door into the garage, and you can get into the back of the car. You need to lie down between the seats and I'll put a blanket over you. OK?"

Skye nodded again. She followed him into the garage, and climbed into the back of the car. It was uncomfortable on the floor, and when Buddy put the blanket over her it was hot and stuffy, but she was going to be good. She really hoped that if she was good she might be able to go home. As Buddy drove, she thought very hard. She liked to read Enid Blyton books about the Famous Five. Mummy said she had read those books when she was a girl, and she and Skye would often read them together. She thought about the children in the books. They were all very brave, and she knew that if she was George she would find a way of escaping. She wondered if she would be able to be as brave as her, and what George would do to try and escape. Perhaps if they were in a shop she would speak to the lady on the till, and say, "this isn't my Daddy, he made me come away with him, but please will you take me home to my real Mummy and Daddy?" But what if the lady didn't believe her? What would Buddy do then? He might get angry and hit her or something. Skye had never seen him angry, but she didn't want to imagine him cross. It was very difficult to decide what she should do. And in the Famous Five books they always seemed to have a friend with them. If Skye had a friend with her she could talk to her and think about different ideas of how to get away. (Which friend would she choose? Lucy or Sophie? She decided Lucy would be best, as she was quite brave and clever) Skye was still busy thinking about how to be like the Famous Five when the car stopped, and Buddy opened the door and pulled the blanket off her. They were in a car park somewhere, but there were hardly any other cars around.

"Come on," Buddy said, "You can come and sit in the front now. We're away from the nosy parkers in the village."

Skye walked round to the front of the car, happy to feel the cool air on her face. She thought for a second about just running, but she couldn't see anywhere to run to, and there was nobody else around to shout to. She sat herself in the front of the car. It was interesting to look around after being in the cellar for so long. The leaves were beginning to fall off the trees, and she realised with wonder that it must be almost autumn. How long had she been away? At first she had tried to count the days, but had forgotten after a while. Her friends must have all gone back to school by now. Did they wonder where she was? Or had they forgotten her already? The scenery whipped past, and she looked around her as they came to the outskirts of a big town. Buddy parked upstairs in a multi-storey car park. When they got out of the car he held her hand very tight. Did he know she was thinking about running away?

They went into a few shops. In Marks and Spencer, Buddy bought her some underwear, which was a bit embarrassing, although he did let her choose. Then they went to another shop where he bought her some T-shirts, jumpers and trousers. All the time he held onto her hand, and she had no way of getting away from him. As the day wore on she felt more and more sad and tired. She liked shopping with her family and friends, but this was horrible. She couldn't feel happy about the new clothes. They were no use if she had to wear them in the smelly old cellar. But one good thing happened that day: Buddy took her to a big department store. They rode the escalator to the third floor, where there was a children's' department that had toys and books. Buddy said she could choose some books and comics and, while they were looking around Skye saw a cuddly dog. It reminded her of her toy dog at home, although it wasn't as nice of course. She stood in front of the dog for a long time, letting her fingers wander over its fur, not daring to pick it up, as it would hurt to have to put it down again. Buddy watched her for a few minutes, then asked; "Would you like me to buy you the dog?" she nodded, hardly daring to speak, and he picked it up, saying, "as you've been so good today you can have it as a treat."

"Thank you, Buddy," she whispered, watching his big hands holding the dog so casually as he took it to the till with their other purchases.

She held on to it tightly through the bag as they left the store, thinking of how nice it would be to cuddle the dog at nighttime. Until she came here she had never slept without a toy, and it felt very lonely to be so alone in her bed.

Eventually Buddy led her back towards the car park. They walked past a very big old church where there were lots of people standing around. Buddy walked a bit faster as they went past. Skye wondered if there was someone he knew there. She turned around as they dashed past, and saw that there was a man with a video camera, and people seemed to be looking at him rather than at the church. Did Buddy know the man with the camera? she wondered.

Once they were back in the car, Skye found that her eyes were very heavy, and she was having trouble keeping them open. Buddy had to wake her up to get into the back when they were at the car park again. She was too sleepy to think about running away now. He let her take the dog out of the bag, and she held him to her face as she crouched under the blanket, rubbing his comfortingly soft fur against her cheek as she dozed.

TEN

Rain was lashing against the window as Bonnie cleared away the dinner plates. Autumn had set in now, the days getting colder and shorter with each passing week. Summer had gone straight to her room after dinner, to listen to her CDs and supposedly do her homework. Dan had disappeared into the study, to catch up on his paperwork he said, although she thought it more likely he just wanted to be away from her. She sighed. The ache in her heart never seemed to improve. People were forever telling her that time healed, but it was a lie. She had been walking around with an empty space beside her for two months now, and it was almost as painful today as it had been the night of Skye's disappearance. Almost. Amazingly, she had begun to have mornings when her first thought on waking was not of Skye. Instead she would work her way toward the realisation bit-by-bit, until, all at once, her hand would fly to her mouth and she would know: Skye's gone. How could she have forgotten, even for a moment? But the pain never abated, even for a moment.

Dan had stopped asking her if she was going to go back to work any time soon. She could not bear the thought of returning to the bank now. The notion of her colleagues, all trying to be understanding, made her stomach knot. And the idea of facing customers again, horrified her. She didn't want to do anything until she had Skye back home where she belonged. If she was honest, she didn't like being at home on her own either. The silence pressed around her, and she had nothing to occupy her. She was unable to read any more, her concentration had disappeared at the same time as Skye. Sometimes she would turn on the television and sit in front of it while her mind wandered. She would long for the time when Summer and Dan would return at the end of the day, but once they had been home for ten minutes she wished for the silence back again.

She only left the house now to go food shopping. She had worked out that if she went by car to the furthest supermarket from her house, she was less likely to bump into people she knew. She would scuttle quickly up and down the aisles before racing back to her car.

As she washed the dishes, Bonnie looked out at the driving rain. She hoped that Skye was at least somewhere warm and dry, not out in the wet. She tried to concentrate her mind enough to reach out to Skye. Sometimes she felt that this worked, that Skye could really hear her, but most often she felt as if she was shouting in a vacuum.

Bonnie had had a hard day. She had not slept well the night before, her mind constantly scanning for messages from Skye, afraid she might miss some vital clue in Skye's calling. She had woken late, feeling groggy and heavy with sleep. As always she had made herself get up when Summer did, making a breakfast which Summer tried not to eat. This morning Bonnie had not had the energy to argue, and had let her go to school with only a glass of orange inside her, something which she regretted the instant Summer was out of sight.

The day had stretched before her, empty and frightening. It seemed astonishing to her now to remember that only three months ago she had longed for a day to herself, had looked for opportunities to be alone. She had vacuumed downstairs, and dusted in a desultory fashion. At 10 o'clock the doorbell had rung, making her heart thud and her limbs turn to water. Would she ever again be able to answer the door without this feeling of terrified dread?

On the doorstep was Gillian from across the road, wearing a pair of distressingly flesh-coloured leggings and a too tight blue T-shirt, with a tiny bra underneath which made her look as if she had four breasts. Bonnie managed not to groan aloud at the sight of her neighbour. Gillian was inside the house before Bonnie had managed to say hello, and she found herself following Gillian into her own kitchen.

"Come on, Bonnie!" Gillian exclaimed in her high-pitched voice, "Get the plates out, I've brought us cakes! I know you're not eating properly, so I got cream cakes to feed you up. I know how you love cream cakes!"

Bonnie fetched two plates from the cupboard, glad of the opportunity to turn her back on Gillian. She had never been a lover of cream cakes, as her friends and colleagues all knew. If anybody at work was buying cakes to celebrate something, they always bought a Belgian bun for Bonnie instead of something creamy. She filled the kettle and took two mugs out of the cupboard. She would have liked to lie and say that she was busy and Gillian would have to go soon, but Gillian was so nosy that she knew Bonnie hardly ever went out any more.

Sitting at the table, Bonnie picked at her cake, letting Gillian's shrill squawkings go over her head as she allowed her mind to wander. She had made a big mistake three weeks ago, when in a weak moment she had told Gillian about Skye calling to her. Since then Gillian had been agog for information, cloaked in pretence at caring friendship. She came over at least every other day, wanting to know if Bonnie had heard from Skye, and what she had said to her. Bonnie would have liked to punch Gillian on the nose and tell her to push off with her interfering natterings and gossip-mongering.

My goodness! She thought, what was the matter with her? She was not a violent person at all. She had never particularly liked Gillian, and had often resorted to white lies to avoid her - had even hidden in a shop doorway once to avoid her neighbour. But she had never before wanted to hit her. It must be the stress making her so bad-tempered.

After about an hour, she had managed to get rid of Gillian by telling her that she felt a bit sick and needed the toilet. Luckily this ruse worked - she wouldn't have been surprised if Gillian had insisted on accompanying her to the bathroom.

She had cleared away the cake plates and mugs, and then wandered to the kitchen window to gaze blankly out at the garden. Her stomach contracted with the pain of her current lonely life. She felt cut off from everybody, even Summer seemed to be trailing farther and farther away from her, and Dan was so far distant she felt as if an invisible icy wall had been erected between them.

The doorbell rang again, her heart leapt into her throat, and her knees buckled. She staggered as she turned towards the door, her pulse beating a loud tattoo in her head.

This time it was a slightly more welcome visitor, in the shape of Bill from church. She invited him into the kitchen, where she again filled the kettle, glancing at the clock as she did so. She was alarmed to see that it was almost four o'clock. How long had she stood at the window? It was shocking the way time seemed to expand and contract these days.

"How are you today, Bonnie?" Bill asked.

She nodded, unsure what to say. It would be dishonest to say she was fine, but did he want to know how she truly felt? He seemed to read these thoughts on her face, and smiled and patted her hand.

"That bad, huh?" he asked. Bonnie nodded once more, swallowing over the lump which had risen into her throat.

Bill was somebody who Bonnie knew she could trust absolutely, but she was still unsure how much he believed her at the moment.

"It doesn't get any easier," she said at last. "I'm still waiting for a phone call to say they've found Skye. I'm still walking around with a huge hole in my heart. I just don't know what to do for the best any more."

Bill opened his mouth, but before he could speak she leapt in with, "And don't even think of telling me to think of the family I have left! I know Dan and Summer still need me, but what about Skye? She needs me more than they

83

do, and nobody seems to think about that!" She ran out of steam then, her hands and voice shaking in unison.

"Do you really think that was what I came here to say?" He asked at last. He smiled to soften the words he had to say, "but you do need to try to move forward a bit, Bonnie. I do understand how hard this is for you, and you know that I believe you when you talk about Skye calling you. But in reality there isn't much we can do about that at the moment, other than praying that God will lead you, or the police, to where Skye is and bring her home to you. I don't think that shutting yourself off from the rest of the world is going to help anybody. Do you?" his eyebrows were raised in query, his face turned towards her.

Bonnie looked obstinately down at the kitchen table. What was she supposed to say to him? That she would forget about Skye until the police contacted her again? That she would go back to work and to church like a good girl and act as if nothing had happened? She looked up, to find Bill still looking at her. She shrugged helplessly.

"I don't know, Bill. I don't know anything any more. Don't know how to talk to people, how to do anything except hurt. Don't tell me to go out and talk to people, because I just can't. I've forgotten what to say." He reached across the table and took her small hands in his large ones, rubbing them as if to convey some of his warmth to her.

It was an unsatisfactory visit, which left Bonnie feeling slightly shaken. She understood what Bill was trying to do for her, but she had no idea how to respond. Part of her longed to return to church on Sunday, to see friends and acquaintances who would greet her with a hug, to sit in the church and let the comforting words of Bill's sermon wash over her as he reminded them all of God's love and wisdom. She knew everybody would understand if she cried through the service, and they would not mind if she was unable to join in the singing. Oh yes, she could do that, it would be possible. And yet, at the same time it was impossible. Dan had started to go back to church each week, and most Sunday mornings Summer went with him. It would be so easy for Bonnie to join them, and she knew they would be thrilled to have her company again. She really didn't know what was stopping her, but the weight which had settled around her since Skye's disappearance was too heavy to carry out into the real world.

And so her day had dragged on once Bill had left with the appearance of a dog with its tail between its legs. She had felt sad watching Bill walk up the road, but had quickly shut the door and returned to her solitary home.

Now she finished stacking the plates in the cupboard and made a cup of tea. She took a cup up to Dan, who accepted it with a mumbled 'thanks', not meeting her eyes. Bonnie wandered slowly down the stairs to the lounge. She sat in front of the television, slowly sipping the hot tea. There was something comforting about hot tea, she had decided. Food just sat in her stomach, making her feel sick and uncomfortable - even supposing she had been able to choke it down in the first place. But tea was hot and went down easily, warming her empty insides.

The news came on the television, full of the usual sadness of fighting in the Middle East, a story about a policeman who had been shot in the line of duty, a politician who had had an affair with his secretary. Bonnie sighed at the dreariness of the world she lived in. Footage of the disgraced politician faded, and the newsreader was once more facing the camera, this time to say that Exeter cathedral had decided to start charging admission during the week, which had caused local controversy. Bonnie and Dan had planned to take the girls to visit Exeter when they were in Devon. Dan had studied at Exeter University, and always remembered it fondly. Of course, events had overtaken them, and they had never got to the city. Bonnie watched idly as the camera focused on a reporter in front of the cathedral, surrounded by cross locals. Behind him a man hurried by, holding a child by the hand. The child, like most children she saw these days, looked a bit like Skye. As they reached the limit of the camera's range the girl turned and looked straight at the camera for a moment. Bonnie uttered a strangled yell, and stumbled to her knees in front of the television. It was Skye! It was her own daughter dashing past the cathedral, her hair a little longer than it had been, but she had looked straight at her, almost as if she could see Bonnie.

"Dan!! Dan!!" Bonnie screamed, finding her voice at last. She tried to get up from the floor, but her legs were shaking too much to hold her. "Dan! Oh, Dan!" she shouted over and over, until her voice was hoarse, and at last she heard his footsteps on the stairs, not seeming to hurry, as if he had all the time in the world.

Dan put his head round the door. "What is it?" He asked, "Whatever's the matter? You look ill, Bonnie."

"Oh, Dan! Oh God! Dan, on the telly, it was Skye! The news at Exeter, they want to charge admission, and it was her! Dan it really was her, she looked at the camera, it was Skye!"

Dan looked dumbfounded. He shook his head. "Bonnie, I've no idea what you're talking about. Who is charging admission, and what does that have to do with Skye? Are you sure you're all right?"

She shook her head, trying to fill her lungs with air. How was she to get the right words out, to make him understand before it was too late? She took a huge breath, trying to calm her thoughts so that she could make sense. Speaking as slowly as possible she told him what she had seen on the television. Dan stood and looked at her, doubt clouding his features.

"You've got to believe me, Dan! Don't look at me like that, I saw her. Don't you think I'd know Skye anywhere? It was her, she was with a man, and she looked straight at the camera for a moment. We must contact the police and tell them. I'm sure they'll be able to find her now they have proof!"

It took Bonnie over an hour to convince him that they ought to contact John Chambers, their family liaison officer, and tell him what she had seen. Dan still appeared unconvinced, but explained that the police should be able to retrieve the footage from the television company so that they could all see it again. He didn't tell her that it would prove that she was wrong, and the child she had seen would turn out not to be Skye. He didn't need to say it. Bonnie could see it written on his face. But she really didn't care any more. She knew she had seen Skye, and the police would prove it to Dan. Then they would find Skye and they could all be together again. So she sat and waited quietly as he made the telephone call.

ELEVEN

Bonnie was exhausted and dispirited. John Chambers had been kind. He had come to the house and sat and talked to Bonnie and Dan, and explained that it would take a little while to contact the BBC and get a copy of their video footage from Exeter, but that it would be done as soon as possible. They had watched the later news programmes, but the item had been dropped in favour of the terrible news of a bomb which had gone off in a holiday resort in Majorca. Bonnie was ashamed of herself for minding so much, but Skye was more precious to her than the unknown holiday makers abroad.

He had left them soon after midnight, promising to ring the next day to update them. After he had gone, Dan had left the room without a word, his silence eloquence itself. Bonnie wished it was possible for her to go to Exeter herself, straight away, and find Skye. But of course it would be pointless as she would have no way of finding her.

Summer was confused by Bonnie's insistence that she had seen Skye on the television. She was clearly worried that her mother was losing her grip on reality and did not want to spend much time with Bonnie at the moment, preferring to spend time with Sam or her girlfriends. When Skye had first gone missing, Summer had appeared to grow up a great deal in a very short time, and almost mothered Bonnie, making sure she ate, making her cups of tea and running her baths each evening. Now, however, she had lost patience, and was embarrassed by Bonnie's continuing insistence that Skye was still alive somewhere.

Now, the morning after the television had given Bonnie such a shock, Summer was in a sulky mood as she got ready for school.

"What lessons have you got today?" Bonnie asked, hoping to restore some communication. Summer shrugged.

"What are *you* doing today?" she asked her mother, "sitting around watching telly, hoping to see Skye again? Why can't you stop this, Mum?" Her voice was suspiciously wobbly. Bonnie longed to take her in her arms and hold her, but was sure she would be rejected.

"You could try to understand, Summer" Bonnie said. "I know it must be hard for you to realise, but I know what I saw. I'm really sorry if it seems as if I'm a bit crazy, but I know I'm as sane as ever. Really unhappy and scared, and wishing things were different, but definitely not mad."

Summer was looking away from her, her chin wobbling. Bonnie walked over to her, and gently put her arms around her eldest daughter, pulling her towards her slowly and carefully, afraid of rebuffal at any moment. Summer sat stiffly in her mother's embrace for a moment, then a huge sob shook her, and she turned her face in to Bonnie's chest, her arms automatically coming around her waist. They sat like this for a long time, mother and daughter, together.

Eventually Summer sat up, rubbing the tears from her face.

"Sometimes," she said carefully, "it feels as if the only one who matters to you now is Skye. As if I don't count any more because I'm still here." She didn't look at Bonnie as she said this, but ever so casually wiped her face with a piece of kitchen paper.

Bonnie was shocked. Is that how it seemed to Summer? And maybe to Dan as well?

"Oh, Summer! No, no darling, that's not true at all! I'm so sorry if I've made you feel like that. You are as important to me now as you ever were. More so really, because you've been such a support to me. I don't know how I would have managed without your help those first weeks after Skye disappeared. Please don't think that, I love you so very much," and she moved forward to hug her again. As she did so, she noticed the clock on the wall, and realised that Summer would be late for school.

"Tell you what, Summer," she said nonchalantly, "why don't you stay home today? You had a horrible evening, and you're upset now. Why don't you stay home and spend some time with me? I'd like that."

Summer took a moment to think about the idea. She wouldn't be able to see Sam if she didn't go to school today, but it would be nice to stay home with Mum. Bonnie watched these thoughts pass over her face as she turned towards her.

"Yes please, Mum. I'd like to stay with you today. Will you phone the school and tell them I'm ill or something?"

Bonnie smiled. "Of course. I'll tell them you've got a bad headache. I expect you must have a bit of a head after crying so much," and they smiled in collusion as she walked towards the telephone.

***

It turned out to be a surprisingly nice day in the end. Bonnie found that she felt almost happy as she and Summer pottered around together. They did a bit of housework and washing, which reminded Summer that she needed some new underwear and school shoes. Bonnie had been avoiding shops and crowds, but she offered to take her out and buy some new things.

Southend High Street was quiet on this weekday morning, and they wandered from shop to shop peacefully. In Top Shop Bonnie bought Summer some underwear and pyjamas, surprised at how much her daughter had grown in recent months while she had been looking the other way. They visited five different shoe shops before Summer was satisfied with a pair of shoes which were trendy enough for her, and sensible enough to please her mother.

Bonnie decided to treat them to lunch in a cafe, glad of the excuse to sit and rest her aching feet. They walked to their favourite pizza restaurant, where Summer happily chose pepperoni pizza, while Bonnie decided that she might be able to manage some pasta. All she really wanted was a cup of tea, but she knew that it upset Summer when she didn't eat.

"Thanks, Mum," Summer said when their meals arrived. Bonnie looked up at her and smiled. "This has been nice," Summer continued, "it reminds me of when we used to go out together. We always used to go shopping and that, didn't we? Before?"

Bonnie nodded. Before. Ah yes, that golden time, before. She reached across the table and squeezed Summer's hand. "I've enjoyed it too, love. Thank you for staying home with me. It's done me good to be with you." Summer beamed, and Bonnie was overwhelmed at how easy it was to make her happy. "Have I really failed you as a mother recently?" she asked.

Summer looked flustered, and pulled at her napkin. "Well, maybe a bit," she said finally.

"I'll try harder from now on, promise," Bonnie said quietly, "but you must tell me if I'm making you feel neglected, OK?" Summer nodded, her eyes too bright.

***

Back at home, Summer retreated to her room, wanting to listen to her CDs. Bonnie sat in the kitchen with a cup of tea, and a lighter heart than she had had for a long time. It had been lovely to spend time with Summer again, and in her secret heart of hearts she knew that she would soon have Skye back with her, now that she could prove that she was alive. To think that Skye had been in Exeter yesterday! Why, she must be there now! Bonnie could go to the town herself, and she might even bump into her! She did wonder who the man was. Last night she had been so overwhelmed to see Skye that she had given no thought to the man she was with, but now it began to niggle at her. There was something vaguely familiar about the man, as if she had seen him somewhere before. Who was he, and what did he want with Skye? Her mind refused to entertain the worst thoughts, and she wondered if he was somebody who had lost a child, and wanted Skye to replace her.

She telephoned Bill to tell him the news. He promised to pray that Skye would soon be found. He was always willing to listen to Bonnie when she talked about Skye, which was refreshingly different to just about everybody else she knew.

John Chambers did not telephone until almost three o'clock, and when he did Bonnie was surprised at what he had to say: "I've been trying to contact you all morning. The BBC have found the video footage you mentioned," he told her, "We are sending a car round straight away. I want you and Dan, and possibly Summer, to be ready. You will be taken to the BBC, where you will be able to view the video. OK?"

"I'll have to get hold of Dan and ask him to come home. Please wait till he's ready!" Bonnie said, her hands and voice shaking with nerves.

John came to the house with the car, along with a policeman and woman. Dan had for once been easy to get hold of, and Bonnie was relieved to find that he was willing to come straight home. They were driven through the late afternoon traffic, heading for London and the BBC headquarters. Bonnie thought that in any other circumstances this would have been an exciting day out, especially for Summer.

The BBC was not as thrilling a building as Bonnie had hoped for. They were passed through security when John showed his identification, and were met by a man who introduced himself as Dean Page. He led the way to the lifts and up to the fifth floor, and then through long corridors, until Bonnie was sure she would never be able to find her way back to the lifts unaided. Dean led them into a conference room, where there was a large television screen on one wall, and many chairs around a large oval table. Summer wandered over to the window, looking down at the streets below, watching the crowds on the far away pavement mill around like so many ants.

Dean casually inserted the video into the machine, and scrolled through scenes of Exeter cathedral until he reached the point where the broadcast had been made. Everyone sat through the broadcast in silence. Bonnie wondered if they could hear the thumping of her heart, as she waited for Skye to appear on the screen. It seemed a longer time than she had remembered, and she had begun to wonder if she had imagined everything when suddenly, there was Skye and the man, dashing past. Bonnie let out a squeak, pointing at the screen. Everybody watched as Skye turned around and looked at them. Bonnie sat with tears pouring down her face, her hands reaching towards the screen. She glanced towards Dan, and saw shock and recognition on his face. See? She wanted to shout at him. See? I didn't imagine it!

Dan cleared his throat. "It certainly does look at lot like Skye," he said. "But it can't be, can it?" He looked over to Bonnie, and she was surprised to see fear in his eyes. She nodded. Summer was crouched in her chair, the cuff of her sweatshirt sleeve clutched between her teeth, tears flowing down her cheeks. Her brown eyes were wide, the lashes clumped damply together.

John rewound the video, and they again watched Skye rush by. Bonnie peered at the screen. "Those are the trousers she was wearing when she went missing!" she said, although she did wonder at her own surprise - what did she expect her to wear? John glanced over at her, and nodded to the policewoman, who Bonnie now noticed was making notes.

Bonnie felt a huge sense of relief. Now perhaps they would believe her! "Well, what happens now?" she asked eagerly.

John sat back and cleared his throat. "The first thing we need to do is to try and trace Skye's steps after she passed the cathedral. We'll approach the nearby shops, parking areas etc., we'll look at CCTV tapes. Talk to parking lot attendants, anyone who was in the vicinity yesterday to see if anybody spoke to her or saw her. We can put out a missing persons profile in Devon," he said, "and perhaps run an article in the local paper, with stills from this video. Then it's really a case of searching the area. If this really is Skye, we should be able to find some clues soon."

Bonnie noticed that 'if.' Surely now nobody could disbelieve her? She looked at Dan, but he was still staring at the television as if mesmerised.

"Can we keep the video?" Bonnie asked, and was relieved when John nodded, although he did explain that they would need to make a copy first.

"Would you be prepared to put out an appeal on the television to try to get the public to come forward with any information they may have?" John asked as they all stood up to leave. Bonnie was startled into inaction. She turned and stared at him.

"I don't know," she said at last. She looked at Dan, "What do you think, Dan? Should we do it?"

Dan shrugged. Looking at his face, Bonnie could see that he was in turmoil. Until ten minutes ago he had believed that Skye was dead, drowned in the sea in Devon, but now he not only had to come to terms with the fact that his daughter was alive and being kept somewhere away from him, he was being asked to make decisions about whether to talk to the press. Bonnie shook her head at John.

"It's too soon for us to be able to give you an answer," she said, "Can we let you know in the next day or so?"

"Of course," John said, "it would be better, time wise, if we could do it tonight, but we won't do anything until you're ready. However," he looked from Dan to Bonnie and back again, "I really think we need to put out some kind of appeal, get the public looking around them. Is that OK with you?" Bonnie and Dan nodded.

They all stood up then, preparing to leave the room. Bonnie did not want to let the video out of her sight, afraid she would never see it again. But she followed Dean back towards the ground floor and the police car.

Back at home, she shut the door behind them, shutting the world out. Summer ran to her bedroom, her need to be alone evident. Bonnie and Dan stood and looked at each other.

"I'm sorry," Dan said, "it looks as if you may have been right all along and I didn't believe you. I'm sorry. So sorry" He reached tentatively towards Bonnie, and as she moved towards him, his face crumpled and tears leaked from his eyes. He held her tightly as they both cried out their grief.

Mummy! Mummy, can I come home now? I miss you all so much!

Bonnie jerked away from Dan, her heart beating too fast against her ribs, hectic spots of colour highlighting her cheeks. She watched Dan's face, hoping that he too might hear Skye call out to them, now that he was beginning to see the truth. But his expression was as puzzled as it always was when she behaved this way. As if he had no idea what was going on.

TWELVE

Mary Hawkins was worried. Gladys did not seem to be herself these days. Recently she had seemed distracted, and not as willing to gossip as she usually was. It had been their custom to have a cup of tea together at least twice a week, and put the world to rights. But just lately, Gladys had been less available. Even when they were together she seemed as if she was somewhere else. It was very odd.

And then there was that television appeal, for that poor little girl who had gone missing in the summer. Mary remembered how sad she had felt for the family when she had heard the little girl had drowned, but now they thought she was alive, and had been seen in Exeter. That was all very peculiar. Mary had read about it in the paper, and seen something on the television as well. They had shown the little girl and a man hurrying past Exeter Cathedral, and they had frozen the picture to show the girl. Pretty little thing she was too, although she looked as if she could do with a haircut, with her fringe hanging too low over her eyes. The police had appealed for anybody who might know anything, to contact them, and there was a telephone number at the bottom of the screen. Mary had watched, fascinated, as they had enlarged the picture of the man the little girl was with, although it was only a picture of the side of his face. The picture was very grainy when it was blown up, like one of those newspaper pictures made bigger, and it didn't seem to make the man any clearer. But it was very troubling. She couldn't put her finger on it, but there was something about the man. She felt as if she should know who he was. She had even written down the telephone number on the screen, feeling very silly as she did so, just in case she remembered who he was. Which she hadn't, of course; even days later she couldn't think who it might be. She had cut the picture out of the local newspaper, and pinned it on the cork board in the kitchen, hoping it would remind her.

The next time Gladys had come round she had seemed upset by the picture.

"Why have you stuck that thing up there?" she had asked. Mary had explained that she felt exactly as though knew who it was, like an itch that was just out of reach. She had pinned up the picture in the hopes that she would remember if she kept looking at it.

"Well, that's just stupid," Glad had replied, her cheeks pink and shiny, "We all feel like that when we see these pictures, especially when we know this is so close to home. You're just being silly, Mary. You should throw that thing away. It's obviously nobody you know."

And after that she had gone home quite quickly. It really was very odd, Mary thought.

***

The tentative truce between Bonnie and Summer continued as the weeks passed and autumn began to make way for winter. Even Dan had mellowed since they had seen the video of Skye. Sadly no progress had been

99

made by the police in Devon, and Bonnie felt herself again sinking into the quagmire of hopeless depression.

Two days after the video viewing, she and Dan had reluctantly agreed to do a television appeal. It had been a horrendous experience. At any time they would have been nervous about speaking to the press, but in the circumstances, it had been unbearable. They had been taken to a conference room at their local police station, and John briefed them on what to say. Bonnie had felt her mouth growing drier and drier, until she was sure that she would be unable to speak. Dan had looked pale, his jaw clenched in a firm line, his hands knotted into fists.

In front of the cameras, Bonnie felt her resolve desert her. She would never be able to speak. She had forgotten everything that John had told her. She felt the beginnings of a nervous tickle in her throat, and knew that if she began to cough, she would continue to do so until she was sick. Shakily she took a sip from the glass of water in front of her, remembering to sip, rather than gulp. Her hand shook, making the water ripple in the glass, and it rattled a little against her teeth. And then it began. John read a statement, and it was her turn. Bonnie swallowed, gulped, and spoke to the camera:

"We haven't seen our little girl for nearly four months. Somebody, somewhere, has her. We are sure that you are looking after her well, and that you love her, but please, please send her home. She is our daughter and we love her so much, and her sister misses her. Please let us have her back." Her voice failed her at this point, and tears choked her. Dan reached across and held her hand tightly as she struggled to regain her composure.

When it was time for Dan to speak, he did not fare much better; "Please send Skye home," he had said, his voice barely more than a whisper, "We need her back to make our family whole again. Please come home, Skye!" And he put his hands over his face, his shoulders shaking, tears running through his fingers.

***

After the incident with the video, and Dan's dawning realisation of the fact that Skye was still alive somewhere, Bonnie had been filled with bright hope for the future. Skye would soon be found and brought back to them. She had made plans in her head, of how she would keep Skye home from school for a few weeks to reacclimatise her, and to talk through any difficult things she may have had to deal with. Perhaps Summer could also stay home with them, and they could all get used to being together again. And then, after a few weeks, she would send Skye back to her school and her friends, and perhaps she would think about returning to work. Everything would be as before, but better, because they had faced disaster and come out the other side.

Bonnie's mother kept in regular contact, ringing most days for updates on what was happening, and coming round once a week to try and pry Bonnie out of the house for a few hours.

But the weeks had passed without any news. John Chambers was kind and helpful whenever Bonnie called him, but he never had any new information for her. At first, the police had been bombarded with phone calls and letters from people who were convinced they knew where Skye was being held. Bonnie heard tales of definite sightings, and people who insisted they knew who the man was, but there never seemed to be any basis for these allegations. Bonnie failed to smile when John told her of one caller who knew for sure that the man on the video was her neighbour, and he had been acting strangely recently. The police had gone to see the man, only to find that where the man in the video was white skinned with fair hair, this man was clearly Asian. After a few weeks these calls tailed off, and she had found herself drifting towards the video player again and again as the days went by, watching over and over as her beautiful daughter hastened past, vainly hoping to find some new clue each time she watched.

Summer had begun to ask about Christmas; where would they spend the day? What presents could she hope for this year? Bonnie felt sick at the thought of Christmas without Skye. She could hardly bear the idea of shopping for treats and gifts with only one daughter to buy for. As usual at this time of year, her mail had been filled with Christmas catalogues, and she could not tolerate the sight of them, throwing them quickly into the recycling bag before Summer could see them and leaf through them.

She telephoned her mother towards the end of November to ask her advice about how they should spend the day.

"You could all come to me for the day if it would be easier for you," her mother had volunteered, "Sally and Joe and the boys are probably coming here. We could all be together. That might be a bit easier on you than being at home."

Bonnie's older sister, Sally, lived in Derbyshire, and so they did not see a great deal of each other. Her boys, Tim and Mark, were a few years older than Summer and Skye, but the cousins had always got along well enough when they had spent time together. It probably would be easier to be at her mother's house, instead of at home where they habitually spent Christmas day. Bonnie wondered what she would do if she felt the need to go away and cry for a bit, as she could not conceive getting through the day unscathed.

"Oh, Bonnie!" her mother said, "you know where my bedroom is, for goodness' sake! You can just go and shut yourself in there. No one will mind. We're your family. You don't need to be hiding your feelings from us. Let's try and find a way to get through this holiday. Talk to Dan about it, see if he's happy to come here."

"Thanks, Mum," Bonnie said. She felt a little relieved at the thought of going to her mother's. It might even be a bit easier with Sally and her boys there, as the focus would be taken off her and her diminished family. They went on to discuss Sally and her family, and Bonnie's mother even managed to make her laugh as she described the antics of Mark, Sally's youngest son. At fourteen, he was in the middle his GCSE coursework, and was deemed to be highly intelligent, but Bonnie and her mother had always thought he was singularly lacking in common sense. Mark thought himself to be a brilliant cook, and one of his many ambitions was to become a top chef - preferably with his own television series. Bonnie's mother recounted the story of Mark's recent cookery lesson at school, where he had been taught to make apple suet pudding. He had done very well, and had received good marks for his effort. What he had failed to tell the teacher was that when he was tidying up, he had found his unopened pack of suet. Somehow he had managed to make suet pudding without any suet in it.

"The funniest thing, I thought," her mother finished, "was that he served the pudding up to his family, and told them the story after they'd eaten! Sally thought it strange that he didn't want to eat any himself."

Bonnie came away from the phone call feeling a bit better than she had done previously. She would talk to Dan and ask if he was happy to go to her mother's for Christmas.

***

On a rainy Tuesday morning halfway through December, Bonnie plucked up the courage to go Christmas shopping with her mother. They drove through the crowded streets to the town centre. When they got out of the car, Bonnie buttoned up her coat tightly, and pulled her scarf tight around her neck. The town was full of shoppers; mothers with cross-looking children in pushchairs, or being dragged along by their wrists. Pensioners pushed their wheeled trolleys through the puddles, woolly hats pulled down over their ears. Bonnie felt despair as she looked at them. Nobody seemed to be having a particularly good time, and she wondered what the point was. Her mother pulled at her sleeve.

"Come on, love, let's make a start," and she began walking towards The Royals shopping centre. Bonnie followed behind, a feeling of panic rising in her chest.

Her mother pushed open the door of BHS. This was always one of their favourite places to begin shopping for stocking fillers. The store was full of Christmas gifts and trees. Lights flashed and blinked at them as they forced their way through the throng of people, and the air was filled with the sound of jingle bells and Christmas music. Bonnie surreptitiously took hold of a piece of her mother's coat, holding on as she had done as a small child. As they reached the selection of Christmas socks, Alice stopped and turned to her daughter.

"Summer would like these," she said, pointing to a gaudy pair of toe socks with snowmen on. "She said recently that she wanted some toe socks. You could get them for her stocking." Bonnie nodded and picked up a pair of the socks. Her fingers hesitated over a pair of pink fairy socks, which Skye would love. Alice looked at her, biting her bottom lip. Bonnie looked at her mother, her eyes filled with unshed tears, her chin raised defiantly. She picked up the fairy socks, adding them to the basket looped over Alice's wrist. Neither said a word. As they looked around the store, Bonnie saw more and more presents that Skye would like. She feverishly added them to the basket, piling up fluffy teddies, fairy bubble bath, noisy putty, sparkly hair grips. Alice kept glancing at her, but said nothing until they had paid for their purchases and walked out into the cold damp air. She turned then to Bonnie and laid her hand lightly on her arm.

"Are you OK, dear?" she asked. Bonnie nodded and swallowed before answering.

"I can't not buy for Skye, Mum. She's not dead, you know she's not. And maybe she'll be back for Christmas!" Her eyes blazed with hope as she said this, and she felt a prickle of excitement for the first time in weeks. Alice merely nodded, and said; "All right, Bonnie. I just don't want you to get too excited and get your hopes up too much."

"Get my hopes up?" she replied, her voice rising, "Mum! I have to keep my hopes up! Skye has got to come home, I just won't give up on her!" and she turned on her heel, and began to walk away from her mother, leaving her to scurry along behind.

Thirteen

It was cold in the cellar now. Skye knew that winter had come, because she could hear the wind and rain at night, and she was cold all the time. Buddy had brought her some extra blankets and some of his horrible jumpers to keep her warm, but her hands felt cold all the time and she wished she had some warm gloves and slippers to wear. At home she had some rabbit slippers that Daddy had bought her last winter. She thought about them now as she pulled the blanket around her feet to try and make them warm. She remembered as well that Nana liked to knit gloves for her and Summer every year. She wondered if Nana had knitted any for her this year. Last winter Summer had hidden the gloves Nana had made. Skye had seen her hiding them at the back of the cupboard and asked why she was doing that.

"Only nerdy wallies wear gloves their Nans have knitted!" Summer had replied, and the two of them had giggled quietly. But Skye had still liked to wear her gloves. She knew that Nana knitted them because she loved her. She wished she had a pair now.

She knew she had been here a really long time now. She had stopped being so frightened all the time, because she understood that Buddy wasn't going to hurt her. A few weeks ago she had very bravely asked him why he wanted her to live with him, and he had replied that he wanted her to be his friend. He had sounded surprised that she had asked. But not cross.

The thing that worried Skye the most these days was that she couldn't remember home as well as before. She was scared that she would forget what her family were really like, and that then they would forget her. She didn't call to Mummy in her head as much now. Mummy never answered, after all. She had begun to wonder if she had been a naughty girl and Mummy and Daddy didn't want her back. She couldn't remember what she had done wrong, but she was naughty sometimes and made them cross. Perhaps they thought she had gone away on purpose, and they would be cross with her for running off. She wished she could phone them. She thought she could remember the telephone number, but Buddy never left her alone in the house - only in the cellar, and then she thought he locked the door. Once she had heard him go out the front door and start the car. She had waited a little while, then quietly gone up the cellar stairs to the wooden door at the top. But the door wouldn't open. Skye had pushed and pulled with all her might, but she couldn't move it at all, and she had sat on the top step and cried and cried. She had shouted out to Mummy; "*Mummy! Mummy, can I come home now? I miss you all so much!*" But there was no answer. No answer at all.

So she was still here. She was used to the cellar now. She didn't like it any more, of course, but she at least had her toy dog to cuddle at night. She kept him hidden under the duvet in case Buddy decided to take him away one day. She had the books and magazines Buddy had bought her the day they went to town, and she read and read them, until she knew all the stories off by heart. She had become braver and started to explore the cellar. It wasn't very exciting, but she looked around. There was her corner, with the manky old mattress and smelly duvet (and now some extra blankets so she didn't die of cold). Near to the mattress was her pile of clothes. She kept these neatly folded like Mummy had always tried to teach her. She would spend ages folding and refolding her small stock of T-shirts, underwear and jumpers. Buddy didn't do the washing as often as she would like him to, so she had to wear the same things for days which wasn't very nice.

On the wall opposite the mattress was a big wooden box. It had taken a long time before she had been brave enough to go and open the box. She was afraid that there was something important in there, and that Buddy would find out she had looked and be angry with her. She had lifted the lid slowly, trying to make no noise at all. Luckily the lid had not squeaked, and she had opened it up to reveal an old sheet lying on top of a pile of books. Curious, Skye lifted the books up to the light. They were all very old, and reminded her of the annuals that she sometimes was given for Christmas. The books were called 'The Boys Book of Friends'. She opened the first book, and began to read an old fashioned story about boys who were super friends, and who saved each other's lives. There were pictures of these brave boys, wearing blazers and caps, and looking awfully brave and posh. Skye smiled at the pictures. The books were all the same, right down to the bottom of the box. She wondered if maybe they were special old books that were worth a lot of money. But it didn't stop her from taking them out and reading them when she was bored.

To the side of the box was the horrible old bucket which she still had to use as a toilet. She preferred to wait until she was upstairs with Buddy, then he let her use the bathroom. But of course, she often had to give in and sit on the bucket.

On the wall above the box were three shelves filled with rusted old paint tins. Skye had thought about opening the tins and painting on the wall - perhaps keeping track of the days, like people in prison did in the old films that Nana liked to watch. But try as she might she was never able to prise the lids off; they were all rusted shut. And she had forgotten how long she had been here now, so there was probably no point in trying to keep track of the days.

The only other thing in the room was a string line strung across the room, from corner to corner. When Buddy washed her clothes Skye had to hang them up here to dry. Although it had never been said, she realised that this was because he didn't dare put them on the washing line, in case anybody saw and knew she was there.

Now, she heard Buddy coming down into the cellar. "Yoo hoo!" he called out, "Who wants to come to Buddy's party?" Skye smiled at him, when he arrived at the bottom of the stairs.

"Who's coming to the party, Buddy?" she asked.

"Me and you makes two!" he said, "Come on then, time to get moving! Oh, you can have a bath if you like? Bring some clean clothes up with you. You need to look nice for my party."

Skye picked up some clean clothes, and followed him up the stairs. Buddy told her to go and have her bath first, then to come back down again. She scurried up to the bathroom, happily locking the door behind her. She felt the water in the bath - it was nice and warm. She took off all her clothes, placing them in the carrier bag Buddy always left there for that purpose. First of all she used the toilet, grateful to be able to do so, then she lowered herself into the water. If she closed her eyes she could almost imagine herself back at home, sitting in the bath, waiting for Mummy to come and ask if she needed help washing her hair. A tear trickled down her face, and she quickly wiped it away, then ducked under the water to wash her hair.

Once she was clean and dry, Skye put on her clean clothes, glad to be warm and clean again. She picked up the bag of dirty washing, and opened the door to go back down to Buddy. Opposite the bathroom door was a sagging bookcase. She had often wanted to look at the books, and today she could hear Buddy humming to himself in the kitchen, so she quietly walked over and bent down. The books looked old and tattered, but strangely familiar. Yes! They were Famous Five books! She touched the spines gently, feeling homesick as she looked at the well-known titles; 'Five Get Into A Fix', 'Five Have A Mystery To Solve', 'Five On A Treasure Island', Why, he must have every one here!

Skye ran downstairs, and without thinking, blurted out; "Buddy? You know all your Famous Five books? Well, I've read some of them before. Could I please borrow them, if I promise to be very careful?" Buddy looked round at her, a huge smile on his face, his cheeks round and red and shiny from the oven.

"Well, Skye, isn't that funny? I knew we were meant to be friends! I've always loved the Famous Five too. Of course you can read my books. Who do you like best? I always wanted to be Julian!"

Skye giggled. This seemed a funny conversation to be having with a grown up. "George." she said, "I wish I was brave and clever like George".

"Well, I think you are very clever!" Buddy said, "Guess what's for dinner today? Your favourite - pizza!" and he led the way into the living room where the fire blazed in the hearth, the lights were on, the curtains drawn, and the table laid for two. Skye sat there, and Buddy placed a plate of pizza and chips before her. For the first time since she had been taken, Skye felt almost happy. She was clean, eating her favourite dinner, and she was about to be allowed to read her favourite books.

After they had finished, and Skye had put her dirty clothes into the washing machine, Buddy got out some board games. Skye was getting used to this ritual. Almost every evening Buddy wanted to play these games. He would bring them some cola to drink, and bowls of crisps. He seemed to have an enormous supply of games. Some were clearly very old, but some looked brand new. Today he wanted to play Monopoly. Skye was not very good at this game, but he didn't seem to mind. It took a long time to finish the game. At the end Buddy had won, but that was OK, Skye didn't mind, because he was still happy and smiling at her, and he let her use the upstairs toilet again before bed, telling her she could choose one of his books on the way down again. Sleepily she brushed her teeth, and walked back out onto the landing. Oh, the choice! She wanted to read all the books straight away. It was so difficult to choose. But eventually she decided on 'Five Get Into A Fix', because it reminded her of the summer two years ago, when Summer was still young enough to want to play with her, and they had spent a whole weekend playing at being the Famous Five. And anyway, she thought, as she stumbled back down the stairs to her dungeon, saying goodnight and thank you to Buddy on the way, she really was in a bit of a fix.

FOURTEEN

Why was Christmas weather never the way it was supposed to be? Bonnie wondered as she rolled out the pastry for some mince pies. If you believed what you saw on television, in books and on the front of Christmas cards, you would expect frost and snow, and clear starry nights. The reality was that December always seemed to be cold and damp, drizzly and grey.

Bonnie punched out circles of pastry and lifted them into the bun tins. She filled each circle with mincemeat, then punched smaller pastry circles to go on top. She brushed the tops with egg, then placed the pies in the oven, setting the timer for twenty minutes. She filled the kettle before beginning to clear away the debris, brushing the flour from the work surface into her cupped hand before throwing it into the bin. She took a cloth and wiped everything down, then sat down with a cup of tea and a sigh. She was so damn tired. She had decided two weeks ago to behave like a good wife and mother. She would work and work until everything was clean and tidy. She would get everything ready for Christmas. If she said nothing about how she really felt, not to anybody, then perhaps God would reward her and send Skye home for Christmas.

So she had shopped with a list, buying all the things she usually got for Christmas. Tins of chocolate biscuits, boxes of dates, string bags of satsumas, a whole box of nuts, and a box of chocolates. Presents for everybody in the family. Bottles of wine, cans of beer, two litre bottles of cola and lemonade, plus a bottle of cheap champagne for New Year. Why, she thought, anybody watching her would think; here comes a happy mother, looking forward to Christmas with her family! Nobody, not even Dan, knew that inside she was screaming.

The timer dinged, and she stood up and removed the mince pies from the oven, lifting them onto the wire rack for cooling. Two weeks ago she had made the cake, and in a little while she would ice it. Dan had put the tree up in the living room, and she and Summer had spent an entire evening decorating it with the old santas and snowmen who had sat on the tree year after year. Bonnie had refused to let her mind dredge up the memories of Skye helping to trim the tree in previous years. She had smiled at Summer until her cheeks ached, and then they had drunk hot chocolate and eaten cinnamon biscuits as they listened to Christmas CDs. It had been quite a show - Bonnie was proud of herself.

But here it was, Christmas Eve, and there was still no sign of Skye coming home. A tear escaped from her left eye and made its way down her cheek. She took a lump of marzipan out of its packet and slammed it down on to the work surface. Took the rolling pin out of the drawer. Oh God, she missed Skye so much. Shook icing sugar over the marzipan and began to roll it into an approximation of a circle. *I want her back home, where she'll be safe*. Lifted the marzipan onto the cake, then realised she had forgotten to jam the cake first. Returned the marzipan to the work top. *Help me God, I can't do this any more.* A sob escaped her, and she pulled her mouth firmly shut. Finally she managed to finish the marzipan, and set the cake to one side.

"What more do you want?" she screamed at God, banging her fists on the table. "I can't do any more. I really thought that if I was good you would send Skye back home to me. But here I am, and where is Skye? Please, please help me!" and she lay her head on the table, allowing herself the luxury of tears for the first time in weeks, folding her arms over her head to shut out the cold, cruel world.

***

Somehow she got through the following day. Summer came into Bonnie and Dan's room early in the morning, dragging her bulging stocking, the way she had done every Christmas since she could walk. Dan made coffee and brought it to the bedroom, giving Bonnie and Summer a kiss each. He rummaged under the bed and pulled out a small parcel, which he passed to Bonnie. She looked at him, managing a smile. Her fingers felt thick and numb as she struggled with the paper and tape. It had to be some kind of jewellery; the box was so small and square. She pulled off the tape, tearing open the paper to reveal, yes, a small jeweller's box. Unaccountably her heart was knocking, and her fingers shook. She sat looking at the box for a long moment, until Dan said,

"Aren't you going to look inside?" She nodded, and lifted the hinged lid. Nestled inside the velvet lined box was a diamond eternity ring. Bonnie looked at it in wonder. Two years ago she had been envious of a friend whose husband had bought her an eternity ring, but at the time Dan had been unimpressed. She turned to him.

"Thank you. It's beautiful," she said, in a voice which trembled.

Dan smiled gently at her. "It's a clumsy way of saying sorry for all that's happened between us the last few months." His voice was also suspiciously wobbly. "I want you to know that I have never stopped loving you for even a moment, and I never will." He put his arm around her shoulders, and pulled her towards him, kissing the top of her head. Bonnie leaned her head on his shoulder, and smiled up at him.

Summer brought them back to reality by jamming her finger down her throat and making sick noises, which made them all laugh, and they returned their attention to Summer's Christmas stocking and the delights within it.

As Bonnie washed up after breakfast, Dan came up behind her, putting his arms around her waist and pulling her towards him. He kissed the back of her neck, murmuring; "Did you like the ring, Bonnie?" She nodded, her eyes on the soapy plate in her hand. "I meant what I said," Dan continued; "I am so very sorry for all that has happened. I should have taken more notice of what you were saying. If Skye really is still alive somewhere then hopefully the police will find her soon and bring her back here. Then we can all be a family again." He kissed her again, gave her a quick squeeze, then left the room to begin packing parcels into the car to go to Alice's house. Bonnie kept her head down, her brimming eyes unfocussed. That if again. He still had his doubts.

Sally, Joe and their boys had arrived at Alice's house the day before, and there was a buzz of conversation and laughter as Bonnie, Dan and Summer arrived, their arms filled with presents. Alice shooed them all into the lounge, giving Bonnie a hug on the way. Sally looked Bonnie up and down before hugging and kissing her.

"Looks like you've lost weight, Bonnie;" she said with a small smile. Always the big sister, Sally liked to point out Bonnie's small faults.

"It's hardly surprising in the circumstances, is it?" Bonnie replied, trying to keep smiling to take the sting out of her words.

"Well, I think you look as lovely as ever!" Joe said, pulling her into an embrace which brought tears to her eyes.

Presents were exchanged and oohed and aahed over. Dan and Joe ran around refilling glasses, making sure that none of the adults had a chance of getting through the day sober. Bonnie followed her mother out to the kitchen to try and get away from the noise for a while. Alice smiled at her.

"How are you managing, love?" she asked as she basted the turkey. Bonnie wrinkled her nose and shrugged. She was somehow contriving to look as if she was having a good time. It was as much as could be hoped for. Alice patted her daughter on the arm, knowing that anything more would bring on the tears which Bonnie hoped to avoid today. "You're doing really well, Bonnie," she said, "I'm really proud of you."

Bonnie pushed her mother gently on the arm, saying "Ah, you're only saying that." But the two women smiled at each other, love and pride in their eyes.

Dinner was eaten, crackers pulled, paper hats put on and taken off again. More wine was drunk, cracker jokes read out and groaned over. Pudding and mince pies arrived, to moans of "I'm too full!" And through it all Bonnie smiled and smiled and smiled. After lunch the teenagers left the room to watch television and play their new CDs, full of friendly squabbles over who could listen to their CD first. The room was quieter without them, and Sally looked at Bonnie, her head on one side.

"What's the latest news, Bonnie?" she asked, as if Alice hadn't kept her up to date on everything. Bonnie and Dan told them a little of the events of the past few months, as Sally looked on quizzically. When they had finished she said; "I would have thought you could have done more to try and find her. I know I would do everything in my power if it was one of my boys, which, thank God, it's not."

Bonnie was dumbfounded. The ignorant, selfish woman! Sally was her sister, and Bonnie would have supported her to the ends of the earth until that comment. Now she stood up unsteadily from the table and said: "Just shut up, Sally. You don't know what you're talking about, and I'm not prepared to discuss this with someone so obviously lacking in any kind of love and sympathy. How dare you say that to me? What on earth have you got inside you instead of a heart? I'm ashamed to have a sister who could talk to me like that. Sorry, Mum," this last addressed to Alice as she turned and stalked out of the room.

She did as Alice had suggested in their telephone conversation so many weeks ago, and shut herself in her mother's bedroom. She paced back and forth in the small room, her thoughts whirring as she fumed. Bloody Sally! How dare she be so high and mighty? What did she know? Who did she think she was?

At last Dan knocked on the door to ask if she was ready to go home. It was very late, and Bonnie would have been happy to leave hours earlier. Everybody hugged and kissed and said thank you and goodnight and see you soon. Except Sally and Bonnie. And finally Alice's door closed behind them, and it was just the three of them outside in the cold, piling into the chilly car with their bags of gifts. Dan started the car, and they were on their way home. Bonnie sat upright in her seat, staring ahead at the dark, empty sky before them, willing them to be back at home, so that she could shut out the world once more.

Back in the house Summer stumbled up to bed, exhausted and over-full, wishing she had not drunk the three snowballs uncle Joe had made for her and hoping she would not be sick.

Dan locked up while Bonnie got undressed. She sat on the side of their bed, rubbing her cold feet. She waited for Dan to come into the room, knowing he would not want to find her already asleep. Not tonight. And when he did come into the room she succeeded in smiling and welcoming him into her arms. He held her so gently, as if afraid she would break, and it was all so different to before. Bonnie kept her eyes shut as they made love, as Dan murmured to her, and stroked her, and told her how much he loved her. And she made the right responses, and loved him back, and made him happy this Christmas night.

And once it was over, when Dan lay on his side, his arm carelessly flung over her stomach, his breathing slowing and deepening, only then did she allow herself to cry. The tears flooded her face, running down her cheeks, filling her ears and making her nose itch. Her chest heaved with the effort of crying, and she thought she could feel her heart tearing into pieces.

Nobody had noticed that all day long there had been a Skye-shaped hole by Bonnie's side. Christmas Day had gone by, and still she was not home. Sometimes Bonnie felt as if the rest of her family had simply shuffled up to fill in the gap left by Skye. It had never hurt more than it did right now. And Bonnie had never been more afraid. She did not want this year to end and the next to begin without Skye coming home. Once she had read in a magazine that wherever you were at midnight on New Year was where you would be for the rest of your life. And she was so fearful that if this year ended without Skye coming home, then she never would.

FIFTEEN

Skye was in a bad mood. Last night Buddy had not come down to ask her to come and have dinner with him, or to play any games. She had not realised how much she looked forward to these times with Buddy. It meant that she got to leave the cellar for a few hours, and have a warm meal and use the bathroom. She couldn't understand why he hadn't come down yesterday - it was the first time this had happened. At first Skye had thought that she must have misunderstood what time it was, but she had waited and waited, and he hadn't come. So now she was cross and scared. She wondered if he would forget about her now, and leave her down here without any food or water. Maybe she had made him cross by not playing scrabble well enough the night before, or by asking too often to borrow his books or have a bath. Or something. What if he never came again? She would starve down here, and nobody would know where she was. There was nothing to eat, and she had not had any dinner, and she was really hungry now. She tried hard not to cry, but it was getting more and more difficult to be brave.

She watched the day get lighter around the boarded up window. It must be past breakfast time now. Her stomach rumbled in agreement. She took a sip of the water that was left in her water bottle, trying to make it last.

She looked at the latest Famous Five book which Buddy had lent her. She wondered what the Famous Five would do if they were her. They would probably manage to find a way out of the cellar, ring the police and Mummy, and get saved. As if *that* was going to happen. She pushed the book away, thinking 'Stupid George. Stupid Julian.' She picked up her toy dog and hugged him, stroking his tail with her thumb and forefinger, trying to ignore the rumblings of her stomach. Suddenly she had a thought. What if Buddy had left the cellar door unlocked for once? She ran up the stairs and grabbed the door handle, turning it quickly to right and left. Nothing. It wouldn't move at all, just like before. She wished she had a hair pin, as people in books always somehow opened locks that way, but she didn't even really know what a hair pin was. She walked back down the stairs, wondering what she should do now.

Back on her mattress Skye again picked up her dog, and lay down, pulling the duvet around her for warmth.

She must have dozed off, because suddenly she heard the cellar door opening, and Buddy coming down the stairs. She sat up and glared at him.

"Where have you been?" she asked, cross tears stinging her eyes. "I waited and you didn't come and I haven't had anything to eat for ages."

Buddy looked embarrassed. "Do you know what day it is?" he asked her.

"Of course I don't know!" she said, her face red and angry, "How could I know when I'm shut in the cellar?"

"Well, today is the 26th December - Boxing Day!" Buddy said, "So yesterday was Christmas, and I had to go and see my mother. She would have wondered where I was if I didn't go. I would have been in trouble!" and he giggled, like a big, fat, stupid boy.

Skye was amazed at how angry she was, she didn't think she had ever been so cross with anybody in her life before. "What about me?" she shouted at him. "What about *my* Christmas with *my* Mummy? Where are *my* presents and *my* Christmas dinner? You made me be hungry all of Christmas Day and today. That's not fair! You're a horrible, stinky old bum-face, and I hate you!" and she turned her face to the wall, sobs shaking her shoulders. She heard Buddy climb back up the stairs and shut the door, and she cried harder, because even if Buddy was what she had said, at least he usually fed her and talked to her, and he was the only friend she had at the moment.

After a long time, Skye stopped crying. She lay down again with her dog, trying not to think about the fact that yesterday had been Christmas. Mummy and Daddy and Summer would have had stockings and presents and Christmas dinner without her. And maybe Nana would have come round for the day and brought more presents and chocolates. *"It's not fair, Mummy!"* she called inside her head; *"Why can't I come home and be with you for Christmas? Don't you want me any more?"*

She heard the cellar door open again, and Buddy's shuffling steps, but she didn't look round this time. Buddy walked over to the mattress and stood there, looking at her. When she looked round at him he looked sad, not cross.

"I'm sorry, Skye," he said, to her surprise. "Would you like to come upstairs now and have a bath and some nice dinner?" Skye sat up and nodded at him. She was too hungry and sad to be cross, so she got to her feet, staggering a little, and followed him up the stairs. In the living room Buddy gave her a glass of milk to drink, which was nice and made her feel a bit less hungry. After that he told her to go and have a bath, and he would have dinner ready for when she came back down.

And when she returned to the living room, all clean and warm from her bath, Buddy had made her a roast dinner, with chicken and potatoes and stuffing, almost like a proper Christmas dinner. Skye felt like crying when she saw it, but she smiled and sat down to eat. The dinner was quite nice, and it was lovely to not feel hungry any more. For afters, Buddy brought her some chocolate ice cream, which tasted good, and then he got out his board games. They played a game of scrabble, until Buddy got bored and said he wanted to play something else. Skye didn't really care. While Buddy went out of the room to find a new game, Skye looked around. Out in the hall she could see the telephone. She wished Buddy would go out of the room for a long time, then she could try to phone Mummy, or the police. She dreamed of having something to put in Buddy's drink to make him rush to the toilet, then she could use the phone. Or a secret pill to make him fall down in a coma. Or a gun to shoot him with. But all she had was a dessert spoon, which wasn't much use really. She knew that if Summer was with her she would laugh and say; "We could scoop his eyes out with the spoon!" and Skye would say "Yuk," and they would laugh. She smiled to herself, thinking about Summer, who was probably the best sister ever in the world.

Buddy came back happy. "Look," he said, "Cluedo! I love this game." He took out all the familiar pieces; the rope, gun, Miss Scarlet, Professor Plum, as Skye watched. She had an ache in her chest, and wanted to cry. She used to play Cluedo with Mummy and Daddy and Summer. Mummy liked to be Miss Scarlet, and she would put on a silly posh voice, and they would all join in, making up silly voices for their players, and they would all laugh. And now she had to play with stupid old Buddy.

They played one game, moving their players around the board and trying to guess who had been the murderer, but things didn't seem to be working out, until Skye realised the problem. You couldn't play Cluedo with only two players! You would always know which cards were in the envelope. Suddenly she was angry again. Buddy was such an idiot; he couldn't even work that out! She stood up, knocking the board over and scattering the pieces over the floor.

"You are so stupid, Buddy!" she shouted, her face red and hot. "You can't play Cluedo with only two people. You need more! You always need more people to play games properly. This is just stupid, stupid, stupid!" and she burst into tears, crying against the ache in her heart, her arms wrapped tightly around herself. She wished she could pick up the little dagger and stab him with it, or shoot him with the gun. Then she would run to the phone and ring Mummy or the police and make them come and get her. She hated Buddy and she wanted to go home to her family.

Buddy stood and looked at her for a long time. She was a bit scared that she would have made him angry, but he didn't do or say anything for a while. When he did speak she was surprised at what he said:

"I didn't think of that, Skye. That's why I need you to be my friend; I need someone clever like you to think of things like that for me. Sometimes two people aren't enough." And he started clearing up the game, quietly putting the pieces carefully back into the box, while Skye sat on the sofa and looked at him, sobs still hiccuping in her throat.

Even when he had put the game away, he wasn't cross. He made Skye a cup of cocoa and gave her another book to read before she went back to the cellar. And when she went downstairs he gave her a packet of biscuits and a carton of orange juice to take with her.

"So you won't be worried about being hungry any more," he said, and, much to her surprise, put his arm around her shoulder and gave her a clumsy hug before saying goodnight and locking the door behind her.

Sixteen

Police today launched a hunt for two 11 year old girls, who went missing from their home in the village of Lynhoe, Devon, yesterday afternoon. Molly Davenport and Lauren Kent, who have been best friends since they started school together at the age of four, were last seen at around 4:30 on Saturday afternoon, when they left Molly's house to buy some sweets from their local shop. Molly's mother, Julie, said that the girls were used to going to the shop together. It was only a few hundred yards round the corner from the house, and the girls knew almost everybody in the village of Lynhoe. The two girls were aware that they should never talk to strangers. Mrs Davenport said, "We are all devastated. The girls are well known around here, and I can't believe that anybody would hurt them. Please, whoever has them, please just send them home."

The police are looking into the theory that the girls may have decided to run away from home, using the money they received as Christmas presents to fund their journey, but Mr and Mrs Davenport, and Lauren's parents, John and Patsy Kent, denied this, saying that their daughters were not the kind to want to run away, and would not wish to worry their parents. The hunt continues today.

Bonnie sat and looked at the newspaper, a feeling of dread prickling up and down her spine. Her heartbeat thudded in her ears, and her hands shook. She went to the bookcase and took out a road atlas, scanning the index for Lynhoe. Turning to the relevant page she traced her finger along the grid markings until she found the village, then looked around. Yes! Lynhoe was only a few miles up the coast from Lynmouth! She just knew that the man who had taken Skye had also taken these girls.

She raced to the phone and dialled the local police station, asking for John Chambers.

"Have you seen today's papers?" she blurted when he came on the line.

"Yes, Bonnie," he replied, "and I know what you are going to say, and I think I agree with you. But we have to leave it to the local police to try and trace these children."

Bonnie was flabbergasted. Shouldn't they go to Devon to find them? But once she calmed down a little, she realised that John was right. The local police knew the area better than the Essex police would do. They would find these girls, she just knew they would! And when they found them, they would find Skye, they would.

But a terrible thought nagged at her. Why, after all these months, had this man decided to take two more girls? Had something happened to Skye? Had he got fed up with her and done something terrible.... no, she mustn't allow herself to think that way. What she must do was to find out what was happening in Devon. Only then would she know where Skye was.

When Dan returned home from work that evening she showed him the morning paper. He nodded.

"I heard about it on the radio." He said, his voice weary. "It terrifies me, Bonnie. Just what is going on there? And what has happened to Skye that he feels the need to snatch two more young girls?" Bonnie could see that Dan was battling tears, and she walked over to where he sat and put her arms around him. She perched on the edge of his chair, absent-mindedly rubbing his back as he held her. Her mind was on fast forward, whizzing through ideas and thoughts which she was afraid to share with Dan. She knew without a doubt that she wanted to go to Devon herself. Now. To find the village of Lynhoe and see where these girls had disappeared. She felt that only then would she find out what had happened to Skye.

The front door opened and then banged shut as Summer came home from her friend's house.

"What's the matter?" she asked warily as she came into the living room. Bonnie explained about the girls who had been taken, watching Summer's face darken into a frown. Her lips compressed into white lines as she listened to her mother.

"What's that got to do with us?" she asked, deliberately obtuse. Bonnie sighed. She could see where this was headed - back down the road to where Summer would draw away from the signs of her mother's madness and obsession. She took a deep breath.

"Think about it, Summer," she said as gently as she could, "These girls were taken in Lynhoe, which is a village just a few miles up the coast from Lynmouth. We *know* Skye is still in Devon somewhere because we all saw her on that news item. It is not just possible, but highly likely, that the man who took Skye also took these girls."

"But what does it mean?" Summer asked, her face a little less stubborn than before. "Why would he take two more girls when he's already got one? Do you think...." her voice trailed off, her lips trembling.

"That's the whole point, love; we just don't know what it means," Dan said, holding his arms out to Summer, who reluctantly moved forward into his embrace.

"There is one thing that it does mean," Bonnie said, watching them turn to face her, "It means that there is a search going on now; just hours after the girls were taken. When Skye disappeared everybody assumed that she had drowned, so they only really searched the sea and the area around it. Surely it is easier to follow a trail while it is still warm?" Dan and Summer were looking at her, comprehension beginning to dawn. "You see?" she continued, "they are searching houses etc. around Lynhoe for these girls, and I think it may be easier to find them because they only just disappeared. And I think that when they find them, they will find Skye too." She beamed at them.

Dinner was a quiet affair that night, with everybody lost in their own thoughts. Bonnie was surprised to find that the emotion she was feeling most of all was excitement. She honestly felt that Skye would be home soon now, along with those two girls, Lauren and Molly. She only wished she was able to do something to hasten the process. If she went to Devon herself, perhaps she would be able to find some detail the police had missed. And perhaps she would be able to hear Skye call to her

131

more clearly when she was near to her again. Recently she had not heard Skye call so often, and it had begun to worry her. What did it mean? Was it that Skye was getting used to her new surroundings, and no longer felt the need to call her mother so often? Or had she given up hope of being brought home again, and so given up trying to call her mother?

Later that evening Bonnie lay in the bath, bubbles up to her chin, the warm water lapping around her. She was unsettled, her mind zooming from one idea to the next, her heart constantly racing. She was determined to go to Devon now, but needed to find a way to convince Dan that it was a sensible idea. She had thought through all the ways of getting there; coach, train, car, and decided that driving would be the best idea, as she would have the independence of the car when she arrived. And she knew that she could not afford a hotel, so she would have to contact the local tourist board to try and find a guest house which would be open in the middle of winter. She picked up the soap and idly washed her arms, rubbing it into her skin, enjoying the lavender fragrance of the soap her mother had given her for Christmas. The smell of lavender reminded her sharply of her childhood. Her parents had always had lavender bushes in the garden, and in summer she and Sally would pick the bright flowering stalks, upending them into brown paper bags, which their father would hang in the airing cupboard until all the flowers had dried and fallen into the bag. Then, in November, their mother would help them to sew lavender bags to give to aunts and grandparents for Christmas. She smiled as the memories of earlier happy, uncomplicated times filled her head, refusing to let her mind dwell on what Sally had said on Christmas Day. There had been no word from Sally since that day. Alice had told Bonnie she was sure that Sally was sorry for what had been said, but Bonnie was uninterested. She would only accept an apology from Sally herself, not through a third party.

There was a tentative knock, and Dan put his head round the door. "Can I come in?" he asked. Bonnie smiled and said, "Of course, silly, I'm not doing anything you've never seen before!"

Dan grinned, and came in and sat on the laundry bin. He picked up the loofah from the side of the bath and began to wash Bonnie's back.

"Mmm, that's nice," she said, her eyes closed. Dan finished washing her back, then scooped water into his hands to rinse her. When he had finished, he moved around to face Bonnie, his hand reaching out to touch her face. She leaned into him, resting her cheek on his palm.

"I know what you're thinking about," Dan murmured into the top of her head.

Bonnie smiled. "I haven't got a dirty mind like you."

"No, you know what I mean," he said, lifting her chin so that their eyes met. "You want to go to Devon now, don't you?" There was no disapproval in his eyes, only concern and a deep love.

Bonnie felt her eyes fill. "Do you really know me so well?" she asked. Dan nodded, his fingers stroking her cheek, his eyes never straying from hers.

"I don't want you to go," he said bluntly, "but I think you probably should. I don't know what you can achieve, but if it somehow puts your mind at rest to be there, then I think you should go."

Bonnie reached up and put her warm, wet arms around his neck, tears running from her eyes.

"I love you so much, Dan Taylor," she said, kissing his neck, "you are really a wonderful man."

Dan said nothing. He lifted her out of the bath and wrapped her in a bath towel before carrying her into the bedroom and shutting the door behind them.

SEVENTEEN

The following morning Bonnie spent a long time on the telephone to the North Devon tourist board. She was unsurprised to find that most of the bed and breakfast houses were closed for the winter, but it didn't help her to know that.

"Can't you find any near Lynmouth that are open now?" she begged the kind woman on the other end of the phone. "I really do need to stay there urgently."

"Wait a minute, I may have something here," the soft Devon burr responded. "Yes, the Cockleshell guest house in Lynton is open. I can give you the phone number of Mrs. Baggs, who owns it. I imagine she will have some spare rooms at this time of year."

"Oh, thank you so much!" Bonnie gushed, "You don't know what this means to me. I can't thank you enough!"

The woman at the other end laughed. "Just enjoy your stay, madam," she said, before giving Bonnie the contact details and ending the call.

Bonnie immediately rang Mrs Baggs, who confirmed in a slow voice that they did indeed have rooms to spare. Would she like a single or a double? Did she want breakfast provided? Bonnie thanked her and booked a single room with breakfast for two nights, beginning the following day. She felt as excited as a child going on a school trip. Her stomach trembled with butterflies and her hands shook. She felt as if she could run around the block, her body was so full of adrenaline.

She rang Dan at work, leaving a message for him to ring her urgently. While she waited for him to return the call, she went to the hall cupboard and took out the large travel bag which always went with them on holiday. She felt a pang as she shook it out. The last time they had used it had been to go to Devon last summer, and Skye's clothes had nestled in there. She took the bag upstairs and searched through her wardrobe for suitable clothes for the trip. She decided on two pairs of jeans, four long-sleeved T-shirts and two thick jumpers. While she was stuffing them into the case, the phone rang.

"Hello?" she answered, her breath coming in short bursts as if she had been running a race.

"Hello, love, it's me," Dan's voice came down the line. Bonnie told him how she had managed to book a room for a few nights in Lynton.

"Do you think I ought to leave tonight and stay at a Travel Lodge overnight?" she asked, "I don't know if it's a good idea to drive so far all in one day." She tried to keep her voice steady and slow, aware that she was gabbling too fast.

Dan agreed, and suggested that she book a Travel Lodge room before leaving home.

"Don't go without saying goodbye to me and Summer, will you?" he asked.

Bonnie was shocked. "No, of course not Dan. I wouldn't do that. I'll have dinner with you when you get home, and then I'll go." Dan offered to come home early, and they said goodbye.

Before Dan and Summer came home there was one secret thing Bonnie needed to do. She took some clean sheets out of the airing cupboard and opened the door to Skye's bedroom. Everything was clean and quiet in there, as if the room was waiting for Skye to return. A few motes of dust hovered in the air. The large collection of soft toys looked down at Bonnie from the shelves as she stripped the bed and put on clean sheets. She plumped the pillows, and placed Skye's favourite teddy on the pillow. "So that it will look welcoming for Skye when I bring her home," she whispered to the room. Skye's favourite toy dog was going with Bonnie, hidden at the bottom of the travel bag. "Just in case," she said to herself. Bonnie sat down on Skye's bed for a moment. The room was so filled with Skye's personality and memories of her that Bonnie rarely went in there, finding it far too painful. She looked around her, at the toys and the books on the shelves. Skye had placed a whole row of *Famous Five* books on the bottom shelf, in easy reach. Bonnie smiled, smoothed the bed and left the room, shutting the door quietly behind her.

Once that was done, she rang Bill to let him know where she was going, and why. As always, Bill was encouraging and concerned. "Keep in touch, Bonnie," he said, "I'll be thinking of you and praying for you. I hope you manage to achieve what you want to in Devon, and I'll look forward to seeing *all* of you when you get back." Bonnie came away from the phone call beaming.

She spent the afternoon planning a nice meal for the three of them. She wanted to leave on a high note, not slope off as if she was doing something wrong. She roasted some vegetables in preparation for cooking a vegetarian lasagne. She debated opening a bottle of wine, but knew that if she drank some she would never be able to drive tonight. Instead she put a bottle of flavoured fizzy water in the fridge. Looking at the contents of the fridge, she decided to make a rice pudding for dessert, as there was a lot of milk to be used up. She was happily stirring the white sauce for the lasagne when Summer walked in.

"That smells nice," she said, looking into the saucepan, "what are you cooking?"

"Just lasagne, followed by rice pudding," Bonnie said, looking into the saucepan rather than at her daughter.

"Are we celebrating something?" Summer asked.

Bonnie turned round to face her, shaking her head and reaching out to touch Summer's arm. "Summer, I'm going to Devon tonight. Just for a few days. I feel I need to be there and see what is going on, see if the police are finding any clues to what has happened to those girls." She paused for breath, looking into Summer's face.

Summer looked at the floor, twisting a loose piece of cotton from her school jumper around and around her index finger. For a moment she said nothing, but then she lifted her eyes to her mother's face.

"I wish you weren't going, Mum. I'll miss you," she said, and there was a tremor in her voice. "But I suppose if you feel you have to go, then you should. You will come back soon, won't you?" Bonnie was touched at this response, which was so different to what she had been expecting. She put her arms round Summer, pulling her close.

"Oh, Summer, I'll miss you so much too!" she said, "and I'll come back as soon as I can, no more than a week, I'm sure. There'll probably be nothing for me to do there anyway and I'll be bored!"

Dinner was a happier occasion that evening. They ate early so that Bonnie could get away before it was too late. Summer and Dan ate heartily, while Bonnie picked at her food, her stomach churning. She wanted to leave now that the time had come, wanted to rush out into the night and hare off down the motorway. But for the sake of Summer and Dan, she had to sit through dinner and say her goodbyes before she was free to leave.

At last dinner was cleared away, and Dan brought Bonnie's bag down to the front door. He put his arms around her, holding her close.

"Drive carefully," he said, "and don't forget to phone us regularly. Remember that we are here waiting for you to come home."

Bonnie smiled. "As if I could forget you!" she teased. She pulled Summer into their embrace, holding them all together for one last moment before walking out to the car. Dan and Summer followed her, opening the car door for her and placing her bag in the boot. They waved and waved as she drove to the end of the road, indicated left and turned out onto the main road. Now that she was on her way, Bonnie wanted nothing more than to turn around and rush back to her family. Oh, her emotions were so contrary!

She had booked a room at a Travel Lodge in Winchester for the night, and hoped to be there before ten o'clock. The roads were surprisingly quiet, and she was able to drive fast on the motorway with no hold ups. She arrived in Winchester just before ten, pleased with herself for getting there so swiftly and finding the place without trouble. Once she had booked in, she flopped on the bed and took out the mobile phone Dan had given her for Christmas.

"Hi Dan, it's me," she said when the phone was answered. "I'm already in Winchester. No problems at all getting here." They chatted for a few minutes, before saying goodnight. Bonnie was tired and wanted nothing more than to have a bath and go to sleep.

She set off early the following morning, after a night's rest which she had not expected. Although she had been so tired, she had imagined she would be too wound-up to sleep, but had slept like a baby from the moment her head hit the pillow, until the sound of someone showering in the next room had woken her just before seven.

The weather was against her this morning, with heavy showers and grey skies. The early morning traffic was heavy as everybody in Winchester had obviously decided to go to work or school by car to avoid the rain. It took a lot longer than she had expected to get to the motorway, and she felt tired and frazzled from negotiating dense traffic in an area she was unfamiliar with.

Once on the motorway, the traffic thinned a little, but the rain increased in volume until it was falling like an oppressive grey sheet from the sky. Bonnie had to have her windscreen wipers on full blast. The speed with which they flew across the wet glass made her feel reckless and out of control. She turned up the volume on the radio, trying to drown out the sound of the deluge thudding on the metal roof of the car.

She arrived in Lynton late in the afternoon, weary and low in spirits. She had forgotten how steep and narrow the local roads were, and wished that Dan was there to share the driving. But she finally managed to locate the Cockleshell guest house, and pulled into the small car park, grateful for the lack of other vehicles. Pulling her bag from the car, she looked around at the familiar landscape. She knew that if she walked to the end of the street, she would be near to the cliffs which looked down on Lynmouth and the beach. The skies were still grey and overcast and it was almost dark. Bonnie could wait until the morning to look at the scenery.

The front door was opened by a plump elderly lady with round apple cheeks and a welcoming smile. "Come in my dear, come in out of the rain. My, you must be tired driving all that way. Did you get wet in the rain? Come in, put your bag down here for a moment. Would you like a nice cup of tea?" An endless stream of chatter followed Bonnie as she was ushered into the warm front room. Mrs Baggs was so kind and hospitable that Bonnie felt tears pricking the backs of her eyes.

The room she was shown to was warm and cosy, if slightly old-fashioned. There was a high single bed, piled with so many blankets and pillows that Bonnie wondered where she would put herself. A slightly battered looking armchair sat under the large window, and an ancient tallboy stood in the corner of the room, next to a washbasin.

"Toilet and bathroom down the hall to your left. There's only one other boarder here at the moment, so you won't have to share. Mrs Smythe uses the bathroom at the other end of the hall. Come and find me if you need anything at all." And with that Mrs Baggs left her to settle in. Bonnie walked to the window. Through the deepening twilight she could just make out the beach in the distance. She was sure she could make out Skye's rock in the gloom, calling out to her through the dark.

EIGHTEEN

The smell of bacon woke Bonnie the following morning. She had spent a restless night in the big bed, unable to sleep until the early hours. At midnight she had given up the struggle, switched on the lamp and picked up her book. She was reading a book called 'New Shoes, Steep Stairs and Sangria' by a new chick-lit writer, Trish Leake. It was the first book which had managed to make her smile since Skye disappeared. She particularly liked the line about 'HRT munchers who look on sex as an excuse for a nice lie-down'. It had actually managed to make her laugh out loud for the first time in months, although she smothered the sound of her laughter in the pillow, afraid she would disturb the other boarder. She had read until her eyelids had begun to droop, then turned off the light and fallen into a fitful sleep.

Now she got out of bed wearily and pulled on her dressing gown before making her way to the bathroom. She quickly showered and dressed prior to heading for the dining room. She found Mrs Baggs bustling around wearing a huge flowered pinafore and carrying an enormous teapot into the dining room.

"Ah, Mrs Taylor!" she exclaimed. "How are you? Did you sleep well? Would you like some breakfast now? Tea or coffee?" Bonnie found it hard to find enough pause to answer, and contented herself with nodding to each question which was directed at her in Mrs Baggs' gentle way.

In the dining room there was one other breakfaster, who she assumed must be Mrs Smythe. She was a tall, thin woman of indeterminate age. Grey hair, tweedy skirt and a pastel blue twin-set. Bonnie smiled and nodded at the woman, receiving nothing more than a slight incline of the head in exchange. Mrs Smythe sat at her own table, and there was only one other place set in the dining room, at a table on the far side near the window. Bonnie supposed this was where she was meant to sit, and took herself off to wait for her breakfast.

Once she had forced down the enormous repast served up by Mrs Baggs, Bonnie returned to her room to decide how to start her search. In her bag she had a map of the local area, and she noted down the route to Lynhoe. She would make her way there this afternoon she decided, but there was an important job she had to do this morning. She looked at her watch, assuring herself that it was after nine, then pulled on her coat and boots and wound a long scarf around her neck.

The rain had mercifully stopped during the night, but the wind had picked up speed, moving on from one tree to the next, bending the leaves as it went, whipping her hair around her face and tossing the smell of the sea at her. She put her hands in her pockets and headed for the main road. Lynton was as she remembered it from the summer, although it felt like a completely different place. In summer it had the busy ice cream scented air of a tourist attraction, but in January it felt like a sleepy country village.

144

Shops were opening as Bonnie hurried towards her destination. She remembered the route clearly from the final days of her holiday. She passed the Post Office on her right and the old school house on her left, and there it was in front of her - Lynton and Lynmouth police station. Bonnie stopped outside the gate for a moment, taking deep breaths and trying to stop the shaking of her limbs. She rehearsed what she needed to say before gathering her courage and walking in through the front door.

A policeman was on duty at the desk, drinking a cup of tea and filling in a form. He did not appear to notice Bonnie as she entered the room. He took a swig of tea and scratched his nose with his pen. Bonnie walked up to the desk and cleared her throat. The policeman started a little and looked up at her.

"Sorry, madam, didn't hear you come in. What can I do for you?"

"Is Wendy Usher in the station today?" Bonnie asked, her voice steadier than she had feared.

"Wendy Usher?" the policeman mused, "I'd have to check the roster. Not sure when she's in. Who shall I say wants her if she is here?"

"Bonnie Taylor."

"Right-o, Mrs Taylor, you take a seat and I'll see what I can find out for you."

Bonnie sat on the uncomfortable bench. She wished she had brought something to read. She opened her handbag and looked inside to see if there was anything of interest in there. She took out her keys and examined them, softly rubbing her fingers over the key ring which

Skye had given to her last year. It was a pink plastic flower, engraved with "the best Mum". She ran her fingers over the words, concentrating on the formation of the italic letters.

She heard footsteps approaching, and looked up into the face of Wendy Usher. She had had her hair cut into a flattering bob, which slimmed her face and made her look younger.

"Bonnie?" she asked now, a puzzled frown creasing her brow.

Bonnie stood up. "Hello, Wendy," she said, "I'm sorry to just appear here like this, but I needed to come." She took a steadying breath before continuing. "I've read about those girls who have gone missing - Molly and Lauren? I think the same man who took Skye has taken these girls. It is just too much of a coincidence that three girls of about the same age would go missing in such a small area. I would like to see where they lived, where they went missing. And if it is at all possible I would like you to try and arrange for me to meet the parents of at least one of them." She stopped and looked at Wendy, trying to gauge her reaction to what had been said.

Wendy sat down next to her on the bench, motioning for Bonnie to sit back down. "Did you come all the way from Westcliff for this?" she asked. Bonnie nodded.

"I really don't know if you can visit the girls' parents, Bonnie," she said, "it would be very unusual. They are enormously upset you know."

Bonnie took a deep breath, determined to hold on to her temper. "I understand Wendy," she managed to say, "I felt exactly the same last summer. Believe me; I know precisely how they are feeling. I would just like to speak to them, and find out what they know, see what sort of girls they are. It would help me, and maybe it could help them too." She sat and watched Wendy, pretending that she was calm, although on the inside she was trembling with fear and rage.

Eventually Wendy spoke, "OK. I'll see what I can do, but I'm not making any promises. You have to realise that this will be asking a lot of these parents." Bonnie nodded, her hands clasped into fists inside her pockets, her nails digging into the soft flesh at the base of her thumbs. "Give me your mobile phone number, and I'll ring you later when I've spoken to the inspector and the parents."

Bonnie thanked her politely, gave her the number of her phone, and left the building. Outside she bared her teeth in frustration. What was the matter with the woman? Did she think that Bonnie would go in and upset people who were feeling exactly as she did? She stomped off down the village street, banging her feet angrily.

After some time she found herself at the top of the cliff lift. Her heart missed a beat as she recognised the cliff-top cafe where her family had eaten lunch last summer. She wondered if she dared go in there to eat today, or if she would find the experience too painful. Dithering outside, she noticed the waitress watching her from behind the counter. This galvanised her into action, and she pushed open the door and walked into the fragrant warmth of the cafe. Smiling at the waitress, she chose a table with a view down the hill to Lynmouth. She ordered a toasted cheese sandwich and a cup of tea, which she ate whilst looking down at the sea.

When she had paid the bill she walked outside, and rounded the corner to the top of the cliff lift. One of the cars was on its way up, and Bonnie waited patiently at the gate for it to arrive. There were a few other people waiting with her, but she avoided their gaze, unable to make small talk. Once in the lift, Bonnie moved towards the front, wanting to stand and look out at the view as they descended. Her heart ached constantly, and she felt as if her insides had been scooped out. At the front of the lift the wind buffeted her, stinging her face and making her eyes water. But that was OK; nobody would be able to tell the difference between tears and watering eyes. She wrapped her arms around herself, hugging herself for warmth.

Down in Lynmouth, she watched as people went about their business, heads bent against the wind. There were few people around, so Bonnie began to walk purposefully towards the beach, unwilling to have others notice her. As she neared the rocks she was aware of Skye's rock ahead of her. She refused to look at it until she was close, her eyes fixed on the ground at her feet as she traversed the wet sand. And then there it was, rising up before her, smaller than she had remembered, but just as red and commanding as before. She rested her palms on its cold damp sides, leaning in until she could lay her cheek against it. Her heart was heavy in her chest, and her stomach was cold and shivery. A loneliness she had never before known filled her. She ought to be at home with Dan and Summer, and even better, with Skye too. She should not be so far away from her family. But, she reminded herself, she was nearer to Skye here than at home.

Bonnie climbed up onto the rock, careful of the slippery wet moss which covered it. On the top she stood as she had done so many months before, scanning the horizon, turning a full 360 degrees to look from the shore to the hills across the water. The sea was greeny-grey, with white capped waves washing in towards the rocks. The sky scowled above her, so leaden that she could see neither cloud nor sun. Behind her was the cave she had found in the summer. She touched her fingers to Skye's necklace, which she had worn around her neck since the police had returned it in October. Descending from the rock was more difficult than clambering up, and Bonnie had to go slowly, feeling for a foothold before letting her weight down.

The cave was as she had remembered, although it was darker inside than it had been back in August. It was gloomy and damp, and Bonnie did not venture far beyond the cave mouth, but stood there, mouth dry and heart aching.

Finally she left the beach and headed towards the river Lyn. She crossed the bridge, assaulted by memories of the days she had walked here with Skye, when they had hurried back to the dry warmth of their holiday cottage to start dinner and put the kettle on. She remembered suddenly, how when Skye was a small child she had so often heard Bonnie ask, "cuppa tea?" that she had thought that was the name of the drink, and would ask people, "would you like a cup of cuppa tea?" Bonnie smiled at the memory, determining that she would make lots of 'cuppas' for Skye when she returned.

Before too long the holiday cottage was before her. There were no lights on, and no sign of life. She wished she was brave enough to walk up to the front door and see if anybody was in, but contented herself instead with glancing through the windows as she walked slowly past. She could see the comfy sofa they had sat on at night, and the funny tiled coffee table with the ugly peacock picture, which had made the girls laugh.

Bonnie walked on past, her footsteps resounding on the path. She followed the river along the way to Watersmeet, stamping out the pain in her heart, feeling that if she just walked hard enough she might be able to block out the pain. The river rushed and tumbled over the rocks by her side, racing past her towards the sea.

NINETEEN

Looking up towards the tops of the skeletal trees, Bonnie realised that the daylight was fading, and if she didn't hurry back towards Lynmouth she would find herself in the dark in this woody area by the side of the river. She reversed her direction and began to hasten back the way she had come.

The bare branches of the trees reached up towards the steely grey sky. Bonnie hunched inside her coat, the collar pulled up around her neck to try and shut out the cold, her hands thrust deep into her pockets for warmth.

She heard the hum of a car approaching, and a red car drove up the lane towards her, pulling to a halt outside one of the cottages. All four doors were flung open, and a family of four spilled out of the car, filling the quiet afternoon with the sound of chattering and laughter and childish giggles. The front door of the cottage was opened and the family hurried inside out of the cold, quickly shutting the door behind them. As Bonnie drew level with the house, the light was switched on in the front room, filling the small front garden with its brightness. The mother of the family came to the window, briefly caught Bonnie's eye, then pulled the curtains shut, the light glinting off her gold wedding ring.

It was almost fully dark by the time Bonnie arrived back at the bridge. She stopped to catch her breath before heading towards the shops. She spied a chip shop with a rectangle of warm light spilling from its windows. Inside there were tables and chairs, and the tantalising aroma of hot chips. Bonnie suddenly realised she was famished, and dug her purse out of her bag. "Cod and chips please, and a mug of tea. Oh, and some bread and butter," she ordered.

"Coming right up, ma'am," said the young man behind the counter. "Sit yourself down and I'll bring it over when it's ready. Would you like the tea now?"

"Ooh, yes please!" Bonnie said, and sat down at a table by the window. In the dark she was able to make out the lights of some of the cottages along the riverbank, as well as houses and hotels further up the hill. They all looked so solid and warm, but Bonnie refused to feel homesick any more, she was here for another couple of days and then she would be home again with her family. Her mobile began to trill in her pocket.

"Hello?" she said, peering at the unfamiliar number on the screen.

"Bonnie? It's Wendy Usher here."

"Oh, Wendy," she said, "thanks for ringing."

"That's OK. I'm sorry it's taken all day, but I finally got clearance from the guv'nor, and I've spoken to Mrs Davenport, Molly's mother, and she is willing to meet you tomorrow morning. How does that sound?"

"Oh, that's brilliant. Thanks so much, Wendy, I do appreciate it. What time, and where?"

"Would ten o'clock suit you?" Wendy asked, and when Bonnie replied, gave her the address and directions.

"I'll see you there," she finished.

Bonnie ate her dinner in a state of happy expectation. Tomorrow! She would be in Lynhoe in the morning, and who knew where after that?

Back at the guest house, Bonnie took a long hot bath, before getting into bed with her book and cup of cocoa. She was terribly tired after all the walking she had done and her legs ached, but she was too hyped up to go to sleep immediately. She sipped the hot drink and looked at the book, until she realised that she had been scanning the pages without taking anything in, while her mind flew over the events of the past six months, and her wishes for the future.

After another of Mrs Baggs' hearty breakfasts, and another nod from Mrs Smythe, Bonnie set out to find her way to Lynhoe. The roads were narrow and winding, and she was afraid of getting lost, but eventually she saw a sign ahead reading 'welcome to Lynhoe', and sighed with relief. Now she just had to follow the directions Wendy had given her over the phone. She picked up the piece of paper they were written on, trying to read them without veering off the road. A right turn, then a left, then there was Molly's road on her left, past the cottages. She could see already that there were police and press around, so she parked in the first available space, outside a cosy looking bungalow with roses growing round the door. She looked at the clock on the dashboard. 9:55. She decided to wait in the car for a few minutes, rather than have to wait outside the house with the press. She was shaky and dry-mouthed, and could think of nothing to occupy her other than picking at her fingernails. As she pulled at the cuticle on her little finger, she saw Wendy's car pull up a few metres ahead of her. Taking a deep breath which threatened to choke her, she got out of the car and called to Wendy before she could walk off without her.

Wendy had obviously decided that Bonnie needed to be given some advice before meeting Mrs Davenport. "Now, Bonnie, she is terrified that she will never see Molly again, and feeling guilty that she didn't take more care of her. Please be careful not to say anything that might upset her."

Bonnie stopped and put her hand on Wendy's arm. "I think that comes under the heading of teaching your grandmother to suck eggs," she said quietly, looking Wendy straight in the eye. To her credit, Wendy flushed before nodding and continuing into the Davenport's road. As they pushed their way through the waiting reporters, Bonnie heard camera shutters clicking, and seemingly random questions being flung at them; "Who are you?" "Any news on where the girls are yet?" "How is Julie?" She put her head down and hurried past, following Wendy up the path to the green front door.

They were led into a small living room, which bore the clear imprint of a family with children. There was a half completed jigsaw on the large coffee table by the window, a couple of Action men sat on a bookshelf, and there were pictures of children on the walls. Julie Davenport was a tall, slim woman with long, dark hair pulled into an untidy pony tail. Her eyes, behind small dark framed glasses, were desperate, and her mouth worked constantly, as if she were pushing something around in her mouth. She gestured for Bonnie and Wendy to sit on the sofa, and sat opposite them in a matching armchair. Bonnie found that her mind was blank, and she had forgotten what she had come here to say. She cleared her throat.

"Thank you for agreeing to see me, Mrs Davenport," she began. The other woman shook her head. "Julie," she said, her voice husky.

"Julie," Bonnie repeated. "Thanks. I'm Bonnie. Did Wendy tell you who I am?" Julie nodded, so she continued; "Well then, you know that my daughter disappeared five months ago in Lynmouth, and I really feel that the same person who has Skye, has taken Molly and Lauren." She looked at Julie, taking in the brimming eyes and working mouth. "I'm not really sure why I wanted to see you, but I thought there may be some kind of connection that we could find together."

Julie sat forward, her hands clasped together, a frown making deep grooves between her eyes. "Where do you think they are?" she asked, "why would someone want to take two or three young girls? What can I do?" Her voice rose with each question, trembling at the edges.

Bonnie leant forward and took one of Julie's hands in hers. "I don't know the answers to your questions, Julie," she said, "if I did, then I would have gone and brought Skye home before this. But I think there must be some kind of connection between the girls that I don't know about. Why don't you tell me a bit about Molly, and maybe Lauren too?"

Julie relaxed a little at her words, and sat back in her chair. She proceeded to tell Bonnie all about Molly's life, from the day she was born, until the day she disappeared.

She explained how Molly was a very kind caring little girl, who was never at all jealous of her younger brother, Ben, even though everybody had told Julie to expect terrible jealous behaviour when he was born. At some point Wendy left the room, and returned with three mugs of tea, which she handed round, smiling gently at Bonnie. As Bonnie listened to Julie pour out her words, she realised that all mothers had the same kind of tale to tell. They all thought their children were exceptionally kind and intelligent, and it was very unlikely that Julie did know anything about what could have happened to her daughter.

"In the paper it said that the girls know almost everybody in the village," Bonnie said when there was a break in Julie's discourse. "Would they talk to anyone who lived here? Was there anybody they were at all afraid of? Or thought was a bit odd?"

Julie thought for a while, then said, "Not really, no. They knew all the shopkeepers as far as I know. They would go to the sweetshop together; they also went to the grocery store for me and Lauren's mum. They sometimes went to the greengrocers, but never the butchers - but that was only because the sight of meat made Lauren feel sick. She's a vegetarian, you know." This last was said with an air of disdain, as though vegetarianism was a form of fussy eating. "They loved to go to the bakers, because they loved the smell. Sometimes went to the post office or the farm shop." She stopped for a moment. "That's it really. I don't know of anybody they were afraid of. They seemed to get on with everybody. They were lovely girls." And she put her hands over her face and cried. Bonnie moved over to sit on the arm of her chair, and put her arm around Julie's shoulders.

"Don't say were," she said, "I know my Skye is still alive. She was seen on TV with a man three months after she went missing, so there is no reason to think your daughter has been harmed."

They chatted for a few more minutes, until Bonnie felt she could bear no more of Julie's raw grief. She made her excuses, thanked Julie profusely for her willingness to talk to her, and headed for the door. Wendy followed her.

"I think I should stay with Julie for a while," she said as Bonnie opened the door. Bonnie nodded.

"It's OK, Wendy. Thank you for arranging this for me. Can I keep in touch to find out what happens?"

"Of course," Wendy said, and patted her on the arm.

Bonnie pulled her coat collar up around her face as she hurried past the waiting reporters, looking neither left nor right as she made for the end of the street. She almost staggered as she turned the corner, assaulted by the same intensity of feelings of terror and helplessness she had felt on the day Skye had first disappeared. She was having troubling breathing properly, her breath coming in embarrassing little gasps which she hoped nobody else would be able to hear. Unable to continue, she stopped for a moment, bent double, her arms folded over her stomach as if to hold in the pain and anguish.

TWENTY

Trying to catch her breath, Bonnie moved over to lean against a wall. She was unsure whether she had the strength to walk to her car, and knew that she was in no fit state to drive. She kept her head down, her chin in her scarf, hoping that if anybody passed by they would not see her helpless tears. She tried to take deep breaths to calm herself, but could only manage the same silly gasps as before.

"Are you all right, dear?" a voice at her elbow made her jump, and she gave a little shriek. "Oh, I didn't mean to startle you, I'm sorry." Bonnie looked up into the eyes of an elderly lady standing by her side, her face creased with concern. "I was in my garden, and couldn't help noticing that you seemed a little distressed. Can I help in any way?" Her genuine concern was Bonnie's undoing, and she found herself sobbing incoherently, her whole body wracked with painful sobs. The lady passed her a handful of tissues, and sat beside her on the wall to wait until the fit of grief had passed.

Eventually she was able to pull herself together a little. "I'm so sorry, sorry," she gasped.

"No need to be sorry, dear, you're obviously very upset about something or other. Now, can I make you a cup of tea? Would that help at all?" Bonnie nodded, looking around to see where the lady had come from.

"Here," she said, "This is my house here. Come on in, I won't bite." Bonnie looked back at the house whose wall she was sat on. It was one of the cottages she had passed earlier, the small front garden had been well loved, and roses grew around the door, pruned ready for the spring. She followed the woman up the short front path and into the little cottage. She was led into a warm, inviting kitchen with a table situated under the window, looking out into the garden. The woman sat Bonnie at the table and filled the kettle before settling it on the range.

"Now, I know you don't know me, but would it help to talk about whatever is upsetting you so?" Bonnie looked at her, weighing everything up in her mind. It might help to talk, she hadn't really spoken to anybody outside her family about her concerns for a long time, so afraid was she of people's reactions to her story.

She took a deep breath, and was about to speak when her eyes were drawn to a newspaper cutting on the pin board on the wall. It showed still pictures from the television news item where Bonnie had seen Skye. There was a picture of her Skye! And a blown-up picture of the man she had been with. She stood up and walked over to the notice board, reaching out to touch the picture of Skye. She peered at it closely, until all she could see were the many little black dots which made up the photo. Standing back a little, she let her eyes wander over Skye's beautiful face. It had been so long since she had been able to touch that soft skin! She turned and looked back at the old woman. Who was she? There was a roaring noise in her ears, and she was afraid she might pass out. "Who are you?" she managed to croak. "Why?" and she gestured to the cutting on the wall.

The woman followed her gaze. "Oh, that," she said, "There was something about that man. I thought he looked a bit familiar, but I can't put my finger on it. Not a very clear picture, is it?" Bonnie shook her head. "My name's Mary Hawkins, how about you?" she continued, "and why does that picture upset you so?"

So Bonnie found herself explaining everything to Mary. The whole story from the day Skye had disappeared until she had arrived on her doorstep today. During the telling, they managed to work their way through two pots of Mary's strong tea, and a few slices of home made fruit cake, and by the time they had drained the second pot, Bonnie felt that she found a friend. Mary was non-judgemental, and nodded when Bonnie told her about hearing Skye call to her, and recalling how she had heard her voice the day she started school.

"That can happen," she had said. "My son, David, was the same. We had a very strong bond, and when he started school the exact same thing happened to me. I had just got home through the front door when I heard him calling me. It was so vivid that I rushed back out into the street, thinking he had followed me home, but there was no-one there. It was the same when he was in hospital having his tonsils out. Mothers weren't allowed to stay with their children in those days, and I would go home and hear him calling to me and crying all evening. It was very distressing for both of us."

Bonnie felt warmth flow through her. Someone truly understood how she felt! She found herself beaming at Mary. "What does David do now, Mary?" she asked.

"Well, that's another story, dear," she said, her face falling. "But the short answer is that he died in a tragic accident when he was twelve years old."

"Oh, how terrible!" Bonnie said, "Oh, Mary, how awful for you. Can I ask what happened? If you don't mind?"

Mary nodded for a few moments. "Very well." she said. "David was my only child. I don't know why. I fell pregnant a few weeks after Paddy and I got married, and we used to laugh about how we would probably have a huge family." She looked sideways at Bonnie. "There was not much contraception in those days, you know." Bonnie nodded. "But for some reason, I just never fell again. But we didn't mind very much," she went on, "he was such a lovely boy. Very bright, and so loving and friendly. Not just to me, mind. He loved his daddy too. He and Paddy used to have some wild times together, playing football and cricket and climbing trees. And the other boys and girls hereabouts loved him too, there was always somebody knocking on the door to ask if little David could come out to play." Her eyes were far away, back in happier days. She was lost in thought for a moment, and then shook herself before continuing.

"Well, maybe it was too good to last. That summer, when he was twelve, Paddy had a few days off work, but we couldn't afford to go away on holiday, so we had some days out here and there." She stopped and looked at Bonnie for an instant. "That day we went on the train to Lynmouth. You could then. Well, no, we got the train to

161

Lynton of course, and the cliff lift down to Lynmouth."
Bonnie nodded, willing her to go on. "David loved the cliff
lift. He would often ask to go to Lynmouth just to go on that
lift. He was fascinated by the fact that it's powered by
water, and was always chatting to the lift operators about
it." She laughed, "I think he would have grown up wanting
to work as an operator on that lift if he could. Anyway, we
all went down to the beach for our picnic, and played there
for a while, and then Paddy wanted to go for a walk up the
hill. We went to the top of the hill, where we could look
over the bay and up into Lynton." Bonnie realised that this
must have been where she had sat the day she had tried
to contact Skye, and her heart jumped in her chest,
guessing what was coming next.

"We were up on the top of the hill," Mary carried on,
"And David was racing around, looking over at the lift,
when he stumbled near the edge. Paddy raced over to
stop him from falling, but his foot caught in a rabbit hole,
and as he reached for David his arm flew out and hit him
on the arm, startling him." She paused, looking down at
her arthritic fingers clasped in her lap. "Well, I expect you
can work out what happened, Bonnie. David fell over the
edge of the cliff, right down onto those rocks you know so
well below. He must have died instantly. But poor Paddy
never forgave himself, and he never got over it."

"Mary, that's the most tragic thing I ever heard,"
Bonnie said, reaching across to touch her new friend's
arm. Mary lifted her hand and grasped Bonnie's, and they
sat that way in silence for a few minutes. Bonnie's arms
were covered in goose bumps, the hairs lifting up in
straight spikes from her skin.

"Well, yes, it was the biggest tragedy of my life. But you know, my dear, we have to move on. Nothing I can do will ever bring my David back, so I have had to content myself with my memories. And I have always been grateful that he died on a day when he was so happy, rather than ever suffering." Bonnie nodded, amazed at Mary's common sense and kindness.

"Shall I make another pot of tea?" Mary asked, looking up. Bonnie laughed softly, and said; "I need to use your loo first, if that's OK?"

"Of course," Mary said, "Through that door there. Bathrooms are all downstairs in these little cottages."

Bonnie went through the door, expecting to find an old fashioned claw footed bath and high level toilet cistern with chain, but was pleasantly surprised to find a modern white suite. The walls were tiled in white, with a border of blue. There was a blue checked blind at the small window, and blue towels hung neatly on a heated towel rail. The overall impression was of cleanliness and warmth.

Back in the kitchen, Bonnie complimented Mary on the pretty bathroom.

"Why, thank you," she replied, her eyes shining with pleasure. "My Paddy fitted it for me three years ago, not long before he passed away. It reminds me of him, and how happy he was doing all the work. He had a massive heart attack a few months after it was fitted, so he didn't get to enjoy it much."

As Bonnie was about to sit back down at the table, she happened to glance at the clock on the wall.

"Mary!" she exclaimed, "Look at the time! It's gone four o'clock! I must get back, and leave you to get on with whatever you have to do."

Mary laughed. "I've got nothing better to do than talk to you, dear. Anyway, I don't want you to go. What have you got to rush off for?"

"Well, nothing really, I suppose. I have to get back to Lynton at some stage, and I ought to eat dinner somewhere."

"That's all right then," Mary said, a smile on her face, "You can have dinner with me. I hate eating alone. It always seems so wasteful to cook for just one."

"Are you sure?" Bonnie asked, "It would be lovely to stay."

"Of course. Now, how are you at peeling potatoes? My arthritis makes it painful for me to do them."

"Ah!" Bonnie said, laughing, "So that's why you want me to stay, so that I can do the difficult bits for you." And she rolled her sleeves up, taking the knife which Mary handed her.

"What, did you suppose I wanted your company or something?" Mary asked, and the two of them laughed companionably as they began the preparations for dinner.

TWENTY ONE

"That was the nicest dinner I think I've had in years," Bonnie said, leaning back from the table and rubbing her stomach. They had eaten chicken breasts in a white sauce which Mary had whipped up, served with fluffy mashed potatoes and garden peas that Mary had harvested from her garden in the summer and then frozen.

"Thank you," Mary replied, "now, what else can I get you? I've some apple pie I made yesterday, and I think there's some cream in the fridge."

"I suppose I could force a bit down," Bonnie said, smiling. She felt lighter of heart than she had for a long time. There was something about Mary which made her feel comfortable and secure. She would be sorry to leave her this evening, as she was unlikely to ever see her again.

As if reading her thoughts, Mary turned to her and asked; "How long are you staying in Lynton?"

"Oh, I have to leave tomorrow," Bonnie replied.

"That's a shame. Do you have to get back for work?" Mary inquired.

"No," Bonnie said, "I haven't been back to work since Skye went missing. I couldn't bear to go and face everybody. They gave me extended unpaid leave, but I have a feeling it won't last much longer and I'll be forced to make a decision about whether to return or hand in my notice." She laughed. "However, to answer your question, the reason I have to go home is that I only booked to stay at the guest house for two nights."

"Do you want to go home?" Mary asked, "or would you rather stay and see if you can find out any more about what happened?"

"Of course I'd like to stay," Bonnie said, "but that's the way things are. I have to go back."

Mary returned to cutting the apple pie, and with her back to Bonnie remarked; "You could stay here with me if you wanted. I have a spare bedroom, and you'd be more than welcome."

Bonnie was dumbfounded. She barely knew Mary, and she was generously offering her this! It would be wonderful to be able to stay in Lynhoe. She could get a real feel for the place, and see if she could find out any more about what had happened to the three girls.

"I don't know what to say, Mary," she said at last. "It is a wonderful offer. Are you sure you'd want me to stay? I wouldn't be in your way or anything?"

Mary inclined her head. "I would be honoured to have you, Bonnie. You are welcome for as long as you want to stay."

Bonnie's eyes filled. Mary was so unselfish and kind. "I would love to stay," she said, "but I'd need to speak to Dan first and see what he thought. He's expecting me to come home tomorrow, so if it's all right with you, I think I'll

166

phone him tonight when I get back to the guest house, and perhaps I can let you know tomorrow?"

"Certainly," Mary said, and handed Bonnie a dish of apple pie and cream.

Bonnie rang Dan on her mobile as she sat in her room at the guest house later that evening. He was surprised to hear about Mary's offer.

"You don't know anything about this woman, Bonnie," he said, his voice filled with concern. "It's not like you to be so rash."

Bonnie laughed at that. "It doesn't feel rash at all," she said. "I just feel so comfortable with her. I feel as if I've known her forever. I'm positive there's nothing to worry about. Please say it's OK, Dan?"

"I suppose you must know best, Bonnie," he said at last. "Just don't stay away too long, will you? We miss you here."

She promised to come home as soon as possible, and went to sleep with an untroubled mind for the first time in days.

The following morning she headed once more for Lynhoe, her travel bag in the boot of the car, and her mind on the days ahead of her. The weather was much calmer than the previous few days, and she was pleased to see the sun peeking through the clouds as she drove along the country roads. It felt like a good omen, as if God was giving his blessing to what she was doing. A shaft of sunlight pierced the sky, and she was forced to put the sun visor down for a moment, feeling the warmth on her face like a loving touch.

Mary opened the door to the cottage, a smile lighting up her pretty face. "Well?" she asked, "have you come to stay?"

Bonnie grinned, "If you haven't changed your mind?"

Mary merely held the door open wider, giving Bonnie's arm a brisk rub as she went past. She showed her upstairs, where there were two bedrooms under the eaves.

"This is my bedroom," Mary said, opening the door to the right of the stairs, to reveal a double bed covered in a flowered pink bedspread which matched the flounced curtains at the window. "And this is your room," and she opened the door on the left. Sunlight filled the small room, lighting on the bed under the window which was made up with snowy white sheets and a blue checked bedspread. The blue gingham curtains framed a view of the hills behind the house.

"It's lovely, Mary," Bonnie said, and impulsively turned and hugged her new friend.

"Oh, go on with you," Mary said with a laugh, but Bonnie noticed that she hugged her back before gently pushing her away.

Bonnie wanted to spend some time exploring the area. She had been unable to do that the day before as she had spent so much time crying and then talking to Mary. Mary agreed to show her around the village, including the place where Molly and Lauren had last been seen. They set out after lunch, bundled up against the cold. Mary slipped her hand through Bonnie's elbow as they walked along. Crossing over the road, Mary led them through the park and past the playground, emerging on the other side of the village. Here were the shops Molly's mother had spoken of; the bakers, butchers, greengrocers, post office, newsagents and grocery store. Mary needed to buy some vegetables, so they went into the greengrocers, where they were greeted by the proprietor.

"Mrs Hawkins! Hello, we haven't seen you for a few days. How are you keeping?" The shopkeeper was a tall, overweight man with receding grey hair. Apart from his Devon accent, he reminded Bonnie of an East End stall holder; he juggled three oranges between his huge meaty hands as he spoke. "And who is this lovely lady with you? Your daughter I suppose? Or your sister? Ha, ha."

"This is a friend of mine. She has come to stay for a few days, Bert. I have no daughters, you know." Mary picked up some potatoes and passed them to Bert, who replaced the oranges in their bin. "Three pounds of these please," she said, "and I need some leeks, cabbage and carrots as well."

Bert quickly weighed and bagged Mary's vegetables, placing them in the canvas shopping bag which she took out of her large handbag. Bonnie took the bag from him, determined to carry Mary's heavy shopping for her. They left the shop and entered the butchers. "I just need some chicken, I think," Mary said. The butcher was another large man, although not as tall as Bert, and quite a few years older. His white hair had almost entirely gone, but there was a large amount of it growing now from his ears and nose.

Outside again in the clean cold air, Mary asked Bonnie what she wanted to see.

"I suppose I'd like to know where those girls were last seen. Would they have followed the same route we took to get to the shops?"

"Yes, I think that's just what they would have done," Mary said, "they were last seen in the newsagents, where they bought some sweets. Mrs Murray says she saw them walking away back towards the park, and she was the last person to see them."

"Apart from whoever took them," Bonnie mused. She stood looking towards the park, wondering what could have happened next. How far did the girls get before being snatched? Did they know the man who had taken them? It would seem unusual for one man to be able to snatch two girls without one of them being able to run away and get help. She told Mary of her thoughts.

"Yes, that's what the thinking has been around here," Mary replied. "They are great friends, those two, and I don't think either of them would stand around and watch the other being hurt, they would have fought back and tried to get help. It does seem most likely that they knew their kidnapper and went somewhere willingly with him. But it is horrible to think that one of our community could have done something so terrible."

Mary looked very sad, standing there facing the park. Bonnie put her arm around her, and asked; "Is there anywhere around here we can get a cup of tea?"

Mary grinned at that. "You're as bad as me for your cups of tea, Bonnie," she said, "you're far too young to be such an old fogey. Look, over there, next to the pub." She pointed over the road, in the opposite direction from where they had come. Next door to the Old Ship Inn was a tea shop. Mary linked her arm through Bonnie's again, and they headed in that direction. The teashop was warm and hospitable, with a wonderful smell of fresh cakes. They settled at a table near the window, so that they could look out at the shops and passers-by, and Mary could tell Bonnie about everybody who went by. The day was getting dark by now, and there were few people around. A young man hastened by on a bicycle, his face pinched with cold, his lips slightly blue.

"That's young John Fogarty there," Mary told her. "He lives a few miles up the road with his parents, John and Celia. He goes to college on that bike of his every day. He's a good lad, but I don't know how he doesn't catch pneumonia in the winter." They watched in silence as an elderly man tottered by with two West Highland Terriers on leashes. He looked unsteady on his feet, and was very slow. "Tom Randall," Mary said. "Poor old thing. His wife died last winter, and I don't think he copes very well without her. He walks those dogs of his every day, whatever the weather, but I don't think he looks after himself too well. His net curtains look as if they haven't been washed since Betty died."

The tinkling of a bell announced the opening of the teashop door, and there was a blast of cold air. A woman of about Mary's age walked in, laden with carrier bags. Her grey hair was pulled into an old fashioned bun, her face at odds with the stern impression this hairstyle gave. Mary stood up.

"Jenny!" she said. She turned to Bonnie and said, "This is a friend of mine, Jenny Smith. She lives just up the road from me. Jenny, come and join us. This is my friend Bonnie, from Essex."

Jenny came over to their table, a big smile on her face. "How lovely to meet you, Bonnie," she said, shaking her hand before sitting down. "How do you and Mary know each other?" Mary and Bonnie exchanged glances, before Mary said, "Oh, our families have known each other a long time. Bonnie was in the area, so I invited her to stay for a few days." She turned to Bonnie. "Jenny used to be the teacher at the village school, so she knows almost everybody who lives in the village."

Jenny laughed at that. "You make me sound like an old busybody."

"If the cap fits..." Mary said, a grin playing about the corners of her mouth. The three women sat for a while, chatting over more cups of tea, Jenny and Mary filling Bonnie in on village gossip.

Glancing out of the window, Bonnie noticed a man come out of the post office, a carrier bag under his arm. He was slightly overweight, but his lumbering gait made him seem much heavier. He walked with his head thrust forward, his bottom sticking out behind him. "Who's that?" she asked idly.

"Oh, that's just Jim, Gladys' son." Jenny said. "Have you met our friend Gladys?" Bonnie shook her head. "Have you seen much of her recently, Mary?" Jenny continued.

Mary's chin dipped as she said, "No, not recently." Her attractive smile had disappeared for the moment. "She's been in a funny mood recently, and doesn't seem to want my company. I honestly can't think of a thing I could have done to upset her."

"I'm sure it's not you, love," Jenny said, reaching across the table to pat Mary's hand, "she's been funny with me too. So would I be, if I had a son like Jim," and they laughed, watching the big man lumbering away towards the park, his receding hair tugged by the brisk wind.

"What's wrong with Jim then?" Bonnie asked.

"Oh, nothing really," Jenny replied, "but at school he was never popular with the other children. He's a bit dim. Not quite stupid enough to go to the special school, but not quite clever enough to fit in at a normal school. Poor thing."

Bonnie sat with her chin in her hand, watching his slow progress across the road. "He kind of reminds me of someone," she said.

Mary laughed at her. "Who's that then?" she asked, "Richard Gere?" And the three women laughed as they paid their bill and made their way back out into the cold afternoon air.

TWENTY TWO

The following day found Mary and Bonnie in the garden, as Mary tried to explain about all the different vegetables and herbs she grew. "This here's my lovely apple tree," she said, fondly patting its trunk. "That apple pie you had yesterday came from here."

"The pastry as well?" Bonnie asked, eyes wide and innocent.

"Oh, go away with you!" Mary laughed, swatting at her. "I'd love to be able to do more, but as I get older and more arthritic it gets harder and harder to do the physical side of it. Shame really, I do so love to eat really fresh veggies."

Bonnie wished she could offer to stay and help when the spring came, but knew that she would be back home by then. If only she and Dan and the girls could come and live next door! She shared this dream with Mary.

"Do you think we could persuade one of your neighbours to move out to make way for us?" She asked, looking around. "That one there would suit us," and she pointed at Mr Ballard's cottage over the fence.

"Now I wouldn't mind that one moving out," Mary said. "There's something a bit odd about him."

"In what way?" Bonnie inquired, peering towards his house.

"I don't really know," Mary replied, "he just doesn't fit in here. He's barely civil most of the time, just grunts if I say hello to him. And in the summer, he suddenly boarded up his cellar windows, which seemed a bit odd. Why would anybody do that? He's just not one of us."

Bonnie's pulse was rushing in her ears. Why would anybody do that? Well, maybe if they had something in their cellar to hide, like a little girl!

"Mary!" she said, her voice sounding hazy and far away. "He might board up the windows if he had a child or children hidden in his cellar. And in the summer is when Skye went missing."

"Oh, my goodness," Mary said, her hand flying to her chest. "Surely not? Surely I couldn't have had your little girl next door all this time and not known about it? Oh, whatever should we do?"

They stood in silence for a few minutes, gazing towards the house next door.

"We could knock on his door and ask him if we could see in his cellar?" Bonnie remarked, realising as she said it how ridiculous this was.

"Oh, yes," Mary said, "We could just say 'we think you have some children hidden away in your cellar. Please may we go and look?'" There was an edge of hysteria in her voice, wavering between tears and laughter.

"Let's go and put the kettle on," Bonnie said, seeing how worried she had made Mary. "Even if he has got them, a few more minutes won't make any difference, will they?"

They returned to the warmth of the kitchen, although both women found their eyes straying to Mr Ballard's house as they sat with their cups of tea. The windows were misted with steam from the kettle, and the light on the outside of Mr Ballard's house shone like fragmented starlight through the condensation. Eventually Bonnie said; "I think we should phone the police. You remember I told you about Wendy Chambers, the family liaison officer? I think perhaps I could discuss it with her, and see what she has to say. Maybe they could get a warrant to search his property or something?"

Mary nodded, and pointed to the telephone in the hall. Bonnie walked slowly towards it, her legs so shaky she was afraid they would not hold her. She couldn't remember the number of the Lynton police station, and had to fumble through the telephone directory to find it. She dialled the number with fingers that felt too thick, and waited while the phone rang at the other end. It seemed an age until it was answered, and Bonnie turned a beseeching look on Mary as she waited. Finally a calm voice answered, and Bonnie asked to be put through to Wendy, giving her name.

"Hello, Bonnie," Wendy's voice came in her ear; "What can I do for you?"

As Bonnie tried to explain, she became more and more aware of the lack of proof of her allegations. Here she was asking the police to investigate a man simply because he was unfriendly and had boarded up his windows. Finally Wendy spoke: "Bonnie, you know we can't go round there just because you suspect the man.

We have to have some real evidence of wrongdoing before we can get a warrant to search his house. Please do try to be patient. We are doing all we can to find the girls."

Bonnie walked back into the kitchen to fill Mary in on the side of the conversation she had not heard. "I don't know what else we can do now," she said, biting her nails. Mary flapped a tea towel in her direction.

"Ruining your nails won't help at all!" she snapped, making Bonnie look up in surprise. Mary's face was crimped into lines which had not been visible before. Her eyes glimmered with unshed tears. Bonnie stood up and put her hand on Mary's arm.

"Don't look so worried," she said, "even if he is the kidnapper; it is hardly your fault, is it?"

"No," Mary said, "no, I know that. But oh, Bonnie! If your little girl has been next door all this time and I've done nothing. I thought it was odd months ago that he boarded up the windows, but I didn't do anything about it. It could be all my fault that Skye has been held so long." A tear ran out of the corner of her eye, making its way down her creased cheek. Bonnie put her arms around Mary, ignoring her resistance, patting her shoulder the way she would one of her children.

"Oh, Mary," she said, her voice quivering, "Don't worry. Whatever has happened, it is not your fault. None of this is your fault at all."

***

Summer came home from school to an empty house for the third day in a row. She dumped her bag in the hall, which was not really allowed and made her way to the kitchen, where she poured herself a glass of orange. Sitting at the table, she looked around at the unfamiliar kitchen. It was funny how different things were without Mum around. She and Dad were keeping things fairly tidy, but the house looked and felt different. She was surprised at how much she missed Mum being here. Things been horrible for the past few months since Skye went missing, but they had been a bit better since she and Mum had started talking again, and it was lonely without her. She hoped Dad wouldn't be late home tonight. He had been good about coming home fairly early since Mum went away, but she was afraid that he would forget and get held up at work. She dreaded the thought of having to sit in the empty house and have dinner all alone.

She walked over to the phone on the wall and dialled Sam's number. They hadn't seen so much of each other recently, and she missed him. She missed the way they would talk for hours about nothing in particular, and the way he would put his arm around her shoulder when she was upset. She loved the way he used to stroke her hair and look at her, as if she were some unusually beautiful object. The phone rang at the other end, and then Sam's mum answered.

"Hi, it's Summer. Is Sam there?" she asked.

"Oh, hello, Summer," his mother answered, "No, I'm sorry he's not. I think he went out to the pictures with Emily."

Summer felt her stomach shrink into a hard ball, and her mouth became dry. What was he doing out with Emily?

She knew Emily fancied him, but had thought it was one-sided.

"Oh, yes," she managed to answer, sounding fairly nonchalant, "I forgot they were going out. Never mind. Can you tell him I rang?"

She replaced the phone and sat staring into space, a single tear making its way down her cheek. So now Sam had left her too. It was true she had not been so attentive lately, but she had thought he understood that things were difficult at home because of Skye. And to think he had left her for fat-thighed Emily! Her heart ached, and she folded her arms over her stomach, holding herself tightly. Oh, she wanted her Mum! By the side of the phone she saw a piece of paper with Dad's writing on it. There was a phone number, with *Mary/Bonnie* written by its side. That must be the number of the house where Mum was staying, she reasoned. Surely Dad wouldn't mind her ringing Devon, even though it was the expensive time of day? Her hand hovered over the telephone, not sure who this Mary was that Mum was staying with, unsure if it was OK to ring her.

Eventually she plucked up the courage to dial the number, and waited through five rings before a quiet voice answered, "Hello?"

Summer cleared her throat. "Oh, hello," she said, "my name's Summer. I'm Bonnie's daughter? Is my mum with you?"

"Oh, yes, dear. I'll just get her for you." And Summer was left listening to the slow creak of ancient floorboards as Mary went off to fetch Bonnie. She heard quicker footsteps hurrying towards her, then the warm comforting voice of her mother, making tears spring to her eyes.

"Summer? Oh, Summer, it's lovely to hear you. Are you all right?"

"Yes, Mum," she answered, her voice thick and wobbly. "I just miss you, Mum. When are you coming home?"

"Oh, darling, I don't know yet. What's wrong? Is Dad home?"

"No, no, he's not back from work yet and I'm in the house on my own and, Mum, I'm so lonely and I wish you were here." And tears flowed, her voice choking on her words, her heart heavy and empty. She felt like a little girl again, alone and scared, and wanted her mum there to comfort her. They talked for a few minutes more, Bonnie trying to comfort Summer down the telephone line, until it was necessary to say goodbye.

Summer sat at the kitchen table, her head on her arms, and sobbed as if her heart would split in two. And that was how Dan found her when he returned from work forty minutes later.

TWENTY THREE

Bonnie watched Mr Ballard's house for the next two days, hoping for a glimpse of the man who may have taken Skye, hoping to see Skye's face at a window, but seeing neither of them. The house could have been uninhabited for all the life that she could see from Mary's back window.

On the third day, Mary and Bonnie went for a walk into the village to buy some groceries. It was an uneventful visit this time - they met nobody Mary knew, and spoke to no one except the greengrocer and butcher, and Gladys' son, Jim in the post office. Bonnie bought a postcard of the village to send to Summer, guilt at abandoning her a constant weight about her shoulders. The lack of people on the streets was partly due to the weather. A damp grey sky hung heavily above the houses, threatening rain which did not come until late in the afternoon, when it fell in a dull sheet which drenched the gardens in seconds. The wind was fierce, whipping the frigid, moist air into their faces as they struggled through the park.

Bonnie was feeling lacklustre and depressed. She wanted to go back home to Summer, wanted to hold her tight and make everything all right between them again, but felt unable to leave Devon without Skye. Feeling torn between the two, she dragged her way back up the road behind Mary, feeling older and wearier than her friend. As they neared Mary's cottage, Bonnie turned to look at the front of Mr Ballard's house. She had spent many hours gazing at the rear of the cottage, but had not yet really looked at the front. His garden was overgrown, last summer's roses hanging brown and dead from their stalks. The grass was far too long, and snarled with weeds and thistles. The paint on the door was cracked and flaking, as it was around the windows. There were three bottles of milk on the front step, and a newspaper hung out of the letterbox. Bonnie stopped suddenly.

"Mary!" She called in an urgent whisper; "Mary! Come here a minute!" Mary turned and looked back at her, her eyebrows raised. She walked back to where Bonnie waited near Mr Ballard's broken and rusted gate.

"What's the matter, dear?" she asked.

Bonnie pointed up the path towards Mr Ballard's door. "Look!" she said, still in a stage whisper; "There's three bottles of milk on the step, and newspapers hanging out of the door. Do you think he's gone away or something?"

Mary frowned. "No. No, I haven't seen him going anywhere. Look, his car's still out there in the road." And she pointed at a smart black BMW which was parked two cars behind Bonnie's Vauxhall. Mary stood looking for a moment, and then came to a decision. She put her shopping down at Bonnie's feet and pushed the gate further open.

"I'll go and knock on his door and see if he's all right." she said, "it's only neighbourly." And she walked up to the door where she lifted the dull brass knocker, letting it fall with a loud crack. She waited and knocked twice more before walking to the front room window and cupping her hand to try and look inside.

"No answer," she said, walking back to where Bonnie waited on the path. "I think we need to phone the police. Something must have happened to him." Bonnie's heart raced at her words. The police would probably have to enter Mr Ballard's house now, and maybe they would find out what he had in the basement.

Back in Mary's warm kitchen, the kettle was filled with water and cups laid out before Mary phoned the police. After some discussion it had been decided that Mary needed to be the one to phone, as Bonnie had spoken to Wendy a few days earlier regarding Mr Ballard. Bonnie sat at the kitchen table while Mary dialled, twisting her wedding ring around and around on her finger and glancing again and again over the fence to Mr Ballard's garden. Nothing moved over there, apart from a few soggy leaves which whirled around in the wind. The kitchen curtains were drawn although it was the middle of the day, and the whole house looked empty and desolate.

Bonnie rested her elbow on the table and her chin on her hand. If she acted as if she was relaxed, perhaps she could fool her body into thinking that she really was. She tried not to listen to the telephone conversation going on a few feet away from her. Her nerves rattled, as if they were all too close to the surface of her skin.

Mary came slowly back into the room, and Bonnie lifted her eyes to look at her friend. She raised her eyebrows in query, and Mary nodded, sitting down at the table with a weary sigh.

"They are going to send the police and ambulance round there as soon as possible, just in case something's happened to him," she said, cupping her gnarled fingers around the rapidly cooling teapot. They sat in silence, watching the bare trees bend as the wind blew across the gardens. The rain began to fall then, hiding Mr Ballard's house from their view for a few minutes as it fell like a metallic grey curtain. Bonnie lifted her hand and rubbed condensation from the window, peering out into the gloom, but it was impossible to see more than a few feet from the house.

Through the noise of the rain they suddenly heard the sounds of cars in the street at the front of the house. They hurried to the front window, where they watched a police car speeding up the road, rapidly followed by an ambulance. Bonnie and Mary grabbed coats and hats, shoved their feet into shoes, and hastened out to meet them. Bonnie hung back as Mary spoke to the two policemen who alighted from the car. She did not wish to appear to be involved. Not until, or unless, they brought Skye out of the house. Her heart was jackhammering, and she leant on the front gate, not sure that she could trust her legs to hold her.

As Mary walked back towards her, the policemen, after a swift consultation with the ambulancemen, walked up Mr Ballard's path, the paramedics hot on their heels. Bonnie and Mary stood side by side and watched the scene being played out before them. The first policeman knocked on the door, waited a few moments, then knocked again. After a further pause he lifted the letterbox, peered inside, then put his mouth to the opening and called out to Mr Ballard, before finally putting his ear to the slot. He then turned to his colleague, walked back two paces, lifted his large booted foot and aimed a hard kick at the door. This had little effect, but when he repeated the action the door flew open, almost causing him to lose his balance. He stood upright, beckoned to his colleague and the paramedics and they entered the house, the door swinging to behind them.

Bonnie and Mary looked at each other, their expressions mirrors of each other's terror. Mary's mouth was pulled into a hard line, her lips almost colourless. She looked her age for the first time since Bonnie had met her. Bonnie could feel the tension in her own face. Her jaw ached horribly, and she realised she had been clenching her teeth. Trying hard to relax her mouth, she put her arm around Mary's shoulder, as much for her own comfort as for Mary's.

Mr Ballard's door swung open and a paramedic hurried out to the ambulance, where he collected a stretcher and a bag of equipment, before hastening back inside the house. Bonnie and Mary exchanged glances. What was going on in there? The hands on Bonnie's watch moved gradually from 2:53 to 2:54, and on to 2:55, and still there was no movement from the house next door. Icy raindrops slid under her collar and down her neck, making her shiver. Her hands were shoved deep into her coat pockets for warmth. She had forgotten her gloves, but was reluctant to go back into Mary's house to get them in case she missed something.

At last the door opened again and the two paramedics came out pulling the stretcher on which Mr Ballard was lying covered in a blanket, a drip inserted into his arm. One of the policemen walked by his side, following the stretcher into the ambulance. Eventually the second policemen came out, shutting the door behind him and locking it with a key. He, however, did not leave straight away, but stood by the gate, watching as the ambulance pulled away, its siren cutting a swathe through the quiet afternoon.

"I'm going to talk to the policeman," Mary said quietly, and walked over to Mr Ballard's gate. Bonnie watched her go, afraid to follow her. Her insides had turned to water, her knees to jelly, and her mouth was as dry as dust. She wanted to rush past the policeman and into Mr Ballard's house, straight down into his cellar to see if Skye was there. How was she to know if they had looked in his cellar? What if Skye was in there, unfed because they had taken her captor away?

Mary was walking back towards Bonnie, a strange expression on her face, as if she didn't know whether to cry or smile. She motioned Bonnie to go into the house, and once inside quietly took off her shoes and coat, rubbing her hands together to restore some warmth. She said not a word until they were back in the kitchen, the kettle back in its familiar place on the lit gas stove. She took a deep breath and said: "He wasn't keeping Skye, or anyone else in his cellar, Bonnie."

Bonnie raised her eyebrows in query, and Mary continued; "The police found him at the bottom of his cellar stairs. Apparently he fell down three days ago and had been lying there ever since. They fear he may have broken his back, as he was unable to get up and help himself at all." She smiled tightly then. "I took the bull by the horns and asked the policeman if he knew why Mr Ballard had boarded over his cellar windows. He was reluctant to tell me at first, but then said that I would know soon enough anyway as the police would be around to do an investigation." She looked at Bonnie, a glint of humour in her eyes as she said, "It appears Mr Ballard is growing marijuana in his cellar. He boarded the windows so that he could use those daylight bulbs to help the plants grow, and so that nobody would be able to see in."

Bonnie stared open-mouthed at Mary. Growing marijuana! She didn't know whether she was relieved or upset at the news. She felt a hysterical giggle rise up in her. Marijuana!

"I wonder if he fell down the stairs because he'd been trying his own crops?" she asked Mary. They locked eyes and began to laugh, tears running down their cheeks as they did so, although it would have been hard to say if they were tears of sadness or laughter.

Twenty Four

"I'll have my secretary draw up the documents and send them to you, and we'll see where we go from there." Dan shook hands with his clients and closed the door behind them. He picked up the internal telephone and asked his secretary to hold all calls for half an hour, as he had notes to write up.

He sat down behind his large oak desk, resting his elbows on it and putting his head in his hands. Wearily he rubbed his eyes, and then ran his hands through his hair until it stood up untidily from his head. He looked at the clock on the wall. 3:15. Far too early to go home. He would love to be able to leave now and arrive home before Summer returned from school. He felt sorry for her, coming home to an empty house every day, and missing her mother and sister so much. He was a useless father to his daughters, he decided. First of all he managed to let Skye disappear from the rocks in Lynmouth, possibly to be drowned or, as now appeared likely, to be snatched by some bastard child abuser. And now Bonnie had disappeared down to Devon to try and find her. He had been happy to let her go at first, thinking it would be only for two or three days, but now she had been gone a week, and he had no idea when she would be back. On top of all that, he hated Summer being alone after school. He knew she was lonely in the house, but was unable to be home for her more than he already was. He and Bonnie had always agreed that, wherever possible, that would be her role. Dan worked long hours as a solicitor, and so Bonnie had always worked part-time hours at the bank since the girls had started school. Until now the arrangement had worked well.

Dan sighed and picked up the family photo from his desk. eighteen months ago they had all looked so happy, sitting on that wall in Wales and eating ice cream. If he had only known how things would turn out he thought, he would have run away with his family and hidden them in a cabin in the Welsh mountains, locking them all in and refusing to speak to anybody. He smiled at his over dramatic thoughts and replaced the picture on the desk. Suddenly coming to a decision, he stood up, picked up his briefcase, and headed for the door. His secretary was typing in the outer office. He stood in front of her until he had her full attention and then said: "I need to go home now. I don't have any appointments for the rest of the day, do I?"

She shook her head, asking, "Is everything all right, Dan?"

He nodded. "Yes, I just need to get back for Summer. I'll be in early in the morning. See you then." And with that he left the building, hurrying towards his car, pulling his overcoat on as he went. He ignored his secretary's stare, which bored into his back as he hastened away.

He arrived home a few minutes before Summer was due. As he walked up the path he noticed that the hall light was on, and for a moment wild hope surged in his heart - Bonnie had come home! But as he opened the door and saw the pile of mail on the mat, he realised that Summer must have left the light on so that she did not have to return to a dark house. His mood plummeted again, even deeper than before, as he realised that Summer must hate coming into an empty house even more than he had previously understood.

Quickly he hung his coat in the cupboard and went to the kitchen, filling the kettle with water and opening the fridge to check how much milk they had. He would make hot chocolate for Summer when she arrived home, then take her out to dinner, rather than heat up yet another microwave dinner. He measured a mug of milk into a saucepan and set it on the stove, turning the gas down low. In the cupboard he found the chocolate powder and Summer's favourite mug. As he was stirring the powdered chocolate into the hot milk, the front door opened, then shut again, and Summer's voice called out, "Mum?" hope rising in her voice.

Dan walked out into the hall, saying, "No, love. It's only me. Sorry. I just thought I'd come home early for you for a change. Is that OK?" Summer nodded and smiled, turning away to hide the tears of disappointment which had sprung to her eyes. Dan strode forward and pulled her into his arms, hugging her against him and murmuring, "It's all right, Summer, Mum will be home soon." She nodded against his chest, but did not look up at him.

"Come into the kitchen when you've got changed," Dan said, "I've made you some hot chocolate." Summer smiled then, and ran upstairs to her bedroom. Dan returned to the kitchen, where he poured the hot drink into Summer's mug, and made himself a cup of tea. He sat at the table, twisting the cup of tea around in his large square hands as he waited for Summer to come back down.

After they had drunk their drinks, they got ready to go out to Summer's favourite pizza house. They drove through the cold wet evening, the wipers swishing over the windscreen, drowning out the soft music on the radio. Summer sat quietly by Dan's side, not speaking unless he spoke first.

When they were seated at the restaurant table and had ordered pizza, garlic bread and salad, Dan decided to take the bull by the horns.

"Are you OK, Summer?" he asked, "do you want to tell me how you feel about Mum being away for so long?"

Summer looked down at her hands resting on the table. She picked up her fork and turned it around in her fingers, not looking at Dan as she answered.

"I miss her. I'm angry that she's not here. I feel selfish for minding, because I know she wants to be able to bring Skye home, and I should be glad about that, but I feel jealous that she's trying so hard for Skye, but forgetting about me."

Dan reached across the table and placed his hand over Summer's. He paused until she looked up at him, then said, "I understand all that Summer, It's OK. I want Mum to come home as much as you do, and I'm going to do something about it."

Summer looked at him, the obvious question written on her face.

"I'm going to ring her tonight," Dan said in answer to her unspoken query. "I'll tell her that you need her here and that it is time she came home. I want her back too, and I'll tell her that." He smiled at Summer then, "And if she doesn't agree, we'll go down there at the weekend and drag her home."

Summer giggled at that, and they finished their meal in companionable silence.

Later that evening, when Summer was ensconced in the bath, which meant that she would be out of the way for at least half an hour, Dan rang Mary Hawkins' telephone number. As Mary went off to fetch Bonnie, he took a few deep breaths to steady his voice.

"Hello, Dan," Bonnie's voice came hesitantly down the line, sounding younger than he was used to.

"Bonnie," he said, "how are you? I haven't heard from you for a couple of days."

"Oh, Dan!" She replied, her voice trembling around the edges, "we've had a horrible time. I thought we'd found out where Skye was being kept, but it turned out to be something else entirely." She continued on, describing the story of Mr Ballard and his fall in the cellar, her voice choking with tears as she explained that her hopes of finding Skye had been dashed. Dan allowed her to talk, and when she had finished, asked when she was coming home.

"I don't know!" she exclaimed; "I don't know how to find Skye. How can I come home and leave her wherever she is?"

192

"You have to, Bonnie," Dan was gentle and firm, "you have another daughter who loves you very much and is missing you terribly. Summer is coming home to an empty house every day after school, she is sad and lonely and she needs you. Bonnie, I need you too. I miss you and I want you to come home." There was a long silence as Bonnie digested his words.

"I don't know what to do," she said finally, her voice small.

"You've been gone a week," Dan said, "it's Tuesday now, so how about we give you till Saturday, then Summer and I will come and meet you. We could come on the train and all drive back together. Summer would like that."

"I'd love to see you," Bonnie said; "Perhaps we could look for Skye together?"

"Perhaps we could all come back home and be a family again?" Dan spoke quietly, but his voice and resolve remained firm. He would not let Bonnie break up their family any more than it had already been damaged. He knew she meant well, and that all she wanted was to bring Skye home, and he really wished that it was possible for her to do that, but had to admit that it did not seem likely. It was better to leave it to the police.

When Bonnie spoke again she sounded sad and resigned; "I wish we could *all* be together as a family again, Dan, but how is that going to happen?"

"I don't know, love," he replied, "But we need you here. Summer needs her Mum. Somehow Skye will be found and brought back to us, but we need you to come home now."

He listened to the sound of quiet sobs from the other end of the telephone line, murmuring; "It's OK, love," from time to time, until he heard Summer come downstairs.

"Summer!" he announced brightly, "come and talk to Mum, she can tell you what we've just been talking about." And he heard Bonnie take a deep calming breath before he passed the receiver to Summer.

TWENTY FIVE

The night seemed to last forever. Bonnie tossed and turned in her bed under the eaves of Mary's cottage. Her legs were uncomfortable and twitchy, so she kicked off the covers, but then she was cold, so she drew the duvet around her again. Her face felt hot and uncomfortable, and she turned the pillow to find a cooler spot. Her brain refused to switch off, and she found herself returning again and again to her conversation with Dan. In truth, she knew that he was right to expect her to return home. She felt horribly guilty about abandoning Summer for so long, and she supposed that Dan missed her, but she wished she could stay here until she had found Skye. She had been so sure that they would find Skye, and the other little girls at Mr Ballard's house, and she was bitterly disappointed with how the day had turned out. She had found herself pierced by an arrow of hatred for the man next door. Strangely, she hated him more for not having Skye hidden in his house than she would have done had he turned out to be the kidnapper. She tried to pray, to find peace with God, but felt unable to do so, she was so filled with bad feelings.

At 2 a.m. she gave up the struggle to try and sleep, and quietly got out of bed, pulled on her dressing gown and slippers and tiptoed down to the kitchen, where she filled the kettle and set it on the stove. As silently as possible she took a mug out of the cupboard and a teabag out of the jar by the side of the cooker.

"Make that two cups, Bonnie," Mary said behind her, making her shriek with fright, almost dropping the mug onto the cold stone floor.

"Oh, you made me jump, Mary!" she exclaimed. "Why are you awake? I hope I didn't wake you?"

"No, not at all," Mary replied, sitting down at the table and drawing her dressing gown around her for warmth. "I couldn't sleep after all that happened yesterday. It's been quite an experience, hasn't it?" She smiled, but her eyes remained sad and haunted.

Bonnie brought the mugs of tea over to the table, sitting down opposite Mary, nodding in agreement.

"I wish I knew where to go from here," she admitted. "I know that Dan is right to ask me to come home, but I wish I could find Skye and take her back with me." Her eyes filled with the quick tears she had been carrying around with her for the past five months. She took a deep breath, and looked away from Mary. Her sight was drawn again to the newspaper clipping which Mary still kept pinned to her notice board. Standing up she once again walked over to drink in the blurry image of Skye. Reaching out she gently touched her finger to her daughter's cheek. *Where are you Skye?* She silently implored. *How can I find you?*

Mary watched her for a moment. "Would you like to go to Exeter tomorrow?" she asked. "If it would help we could go to the cathedral where that photo was taken."

Bonnie turned and smiled at Mary. "That's a fantastic idea," she said. "It will give me a feeling for the last place Skye was seen. Why tomorrow though, why not today?"

"Apart from any other consideration, I think you will be too tired to drive any distance," her wise friend said, "but I would like to ask you something too."

Bonnie nodded at Mary's questioning look.

"I wonder if you would mind if we invited my friend Gladys to come along." Mary continued, "I haven't seen her for a while as I explained the other day. Glad and I used to regularly go to Exeter to shop. She loves it there. I'm not sure if I have somehow done something to offend her, but I thought it would be a nice gesture to ask her. Would you mind very much?"

"No, of course not," Bonnie replied. "That would be lovely. Did you want to phone her today then?"

"No, I would like to go round and see her," Mary said, "I could introduce you. It will be much more personal than a telephone call."

Half an hour later Bonnie and Mary returned to their beds, both feeling slightly lighter of heart, and Bonnie was surprised to find that she fell almost immediately into a deep, dreamless sleep.

At about 9:30 Bonnie half woke, and decided to think about getting up. She was unused to sleeping so late, but then she did not usually spend half the night tossing and turning and drinking tea. She listened to see if there was any sign that Mary was awake, but the house was silent. She lay for a while, enjoying the warmth of her bed, refusing to let her mind dwell on yesterday.

Eventually she got up and quietly made her way down to the little bathroom, where she showered and dressed. By now it was almost 10:30, so she decided that she and Mary ought to eat brunch before setting out to see Gladys. Looking in the fridge, she found bacon, eggs and mushrooms and tomatoes, and set about cooking them. As the bacon was merrily sizzling in the pan Mary appeared in the kitchen doorway, dressed and smiling.

"Now that's a cheerful way to begin the day," she said, "although it does seem a bit late for such a hearty breakfast."

"I agree," Bonnie said, heaping eggs, mushrooms, tomatoes and the bacon onto two plates, "so we are brunching today. If we eat loads now we should be OK till this evening."

Mary laughed, reaching past Bonnie to light the gas under the kettle before sitting at the table. "What's the plan for today then?" Bonnie asked, "When do you want to go and see Gladys?"

"Oh, not for a while," Mary said, "Let her have her lunch first. I think we should go about 2, she's usually in then."

They settled down to listen to the radio until it was time to go out, filling the time with idle chatter about their respective families.

Just after two they put on coats, gloves, scarves and hats before venturing out into the frosty afternoon. The pavements were rimed with ice, and Mary slipped her hand through Bonnie's elbow as they inched their way along the slippery path.

"It's not far," she told Bonnie as they reached the end of the road. "Just round the corner here and it's that house down there on the left - the one with the huge holly tree out front."

As they approached Gladys' house, Bonnie was aware that Mary was breathing a little faster than usual and her cheeks had a hectic flush to them. She squeezed Mary's hand with her elbow, and smiled at her for encouragement. At Gladys' gate, Mary paused for a moment, taking a deep breath and straightening her hat before starting up the path. Bonnie wanted to smile, but realised that Mary must be very unhappy about this pause in her friendship.

Mary rang the bell on the blue front door, stepping back a pace to wait for it to open. She waited a few moments and then rang again, but there was no answer. Her shoulders slumped as she turned towards Bonnie.

"It looks as if she's not in," she said, then something caught her eye and she brightened a little. "I know, her son, Jim, lives next door. The post office is closed on Wednesday afternoons so he should be home. Let's go and knock on his door and see if Glad's there, or if he knows where she is."

Bonnie nodded and followed Mary into Jim's garden and up the untidy path to his green front door. It looked as if he did not take as much care of his home as his mother did over hers. There were pieces of newspaper and polystyrene fast food boxes littering his front path. His brass door furniture could have done with a polish, and the paint around his windows had obviously not been refreshed for a few years.

Mary knocked at the door, and before long they heard the shuffling of slippers coming up the hall. The door was opened, and Jim stood before them, his mouth hanging open in stupid surprise. He was a large man with sloping shoulders and receding hair, but an incongruously childlike air about him. He gazed at Bonnie, his forehead creased, his tongue licking over his lips.

"Hello, Jim," Mary said, and his gaze flickered towards her.

"Oh! Hello, Mrs Hawkins," he said, and then stood there, looking from one to the other of them.

"Jim, I haven't seen your mother for a few weeks. Is she all right?"

Jim thought about this for a moment. "Yes, Mrs Hawkins, she's well, I think," he said finally.

Mary took a deep breath, "Is she here? She doesn't seem to be at home."

"No," he said, his eyes opening wide, "why would she be here?"

"Well, I don't know," Mary said, trying to keep the exasperation out of her voice, "I thought she might have come to see you or something."

"Oh, no, she hasn't. I expect she's busy." Jim turned suddenly, and then looked back at Bonnie, something like fear passing over his face.

"I've got to go now," he said quickly, and began to shut the door.

Mary gently reached out her hand to stay him, before saying, "Would you ask your mother to ring me please? When you see her?"

"Yes, Mrs Hawkins," Jim said, his eyes downcast, and he continued to shut the door on them.

Mary straightened her gloves, giving Bonnie a watery smile.

"It looks as if it's just you and me for Exeter tomorrow," she said.

"I couldn't think of nicer company," Bonnie said, holding her arm out for Mary to hold on to, and they carefully picked their way back to Mary's warm cottage.

TWENTY SIX

Thursday morning was bright, sunny and frosty. Mary and Bonnie were up early for their trip to Exeter. Bonnie was a bit nervous about driving to Exeter on the frosty roads, but was determined that Mary should not know.

They left Mary's house soon after 8:30, spent a little time scraping ice off the car, but were soon on their way. Bonnie drove carefully over the icy roads, but found that conditions were nowhere near as bad as she had feared. Mary was map reader, and they had no trouble finding the roads they needed. When they arrived in Exeter only an hour after leaving Lynhoe, Bonnie felt very proud of herself. They parked in the first multi-storey car park they came to, and were pleasantly surprised to find it relatively empty.

Going down in the lift, Bonnie asked, "Where to first?"

"How about a hot drink?" Mary asked, smiling.

Bonnie laughed. "Now that's the best idea I've heard all morning!" They found a tea room, where they settled themselves at a table near the window, a pot of tea between them.

"I know where the Cathedral is," Mary volunteered, "is there anywhere else you'd like to go while we're here? It seems a shame to come so far and only look at the Cathedral."

Bonnie thought for a moment. She really had no idea where to go. She wished she could go wherever Skye had gone the day she was here, but where would that be? And where was Skye now? She felt that in the past few days she had been running down blind alleyways, thinking she knew where she was going, but constantly coming up against brick walls. Skye must be somewhere - she could not have simply disappeared.

"If you were a kidnapper," she began, looking at Mary, "What would make you venture out into a busy city with the child you had taken? He is obviously not casually taking Skye, and perhaps Molly and Lauren, out and about wherever he goes, or he would have been caught by now. Why would he come to Exeter?"

Mary looked thoughtful, her head on one side as she idly stirred her tea. Her finger drummed a silent tattoo on her bottom lip as she pondered Bonnie's question.

"I can only suppose," she ventured, "that they needed to buy something. A bit of a simplistic view, I know, but if he's a man on his own, there must be things a little girl needs that he wouldn't have."

"Like what?" Bonnie wondered.

"Well, clothes, I suppose."

"But he could buy them on his own. He wouldn't need to take Skye out with him for that, surely?"

"Perhaps he didn't know what to buy? Or what size? Oh, I don't know, Bonnie, but I can't think of any other reason to do something that would be so potentially dangerous to him."

Bonnie nodded. It made some kind of sense, she supposed. She certainly couldn't think of any other reason.

"OK," she said, suddenly decisive, "we'll go to any shops we can find which sell children's clothes. I could show shop assistants a photo of Skye and ask if they recognise her."

To her surprise, Mary laughed. "Bonnie, there are hundreds of children's clothes shops in Exeter; it could take us a week." Seeing Bonnie's crestfallen expression, she went on; "But we could start with the most obvious ones - the bigger department stores. If I didn't want to be spotted, I imagine I would go to bigger rather than smaller shops. You could go unnoticed in the crowd that way."

Out in the cold street they headed towards the main shopping centre, Mary leading the way. As they walked, Bonnie could see what Mary meant - almost every other shop seemed to sell children's clothes. She felt a bit lost at the sight of them all. Skye would love it here if she was with her family, not some weird man. And Summer - she would love it too, she was a shopaholic. Oh, what was she doing here? Her heart was hammering, and a cold sweat was breaking out on her body. Her chest felt constricted, as if somebody was pulling a tight band around her lungs. She felt a gentle pull on her elbow, and looked round to see Mary gazing at her, her face burdened with consternation. As she was opening her mouth to speak, Bonnie quickly said, "I'm OK, Mary. Just anxious and sad. In the nicest way I wish I wasn't here."

Mary nodded. "Are you sure you want to go on with this, Bonnie?"

"Yes. Thank you for asking, Mary, but I want to do this."

Mary nodded, relief clearing her face, and they carried on towards a large department store ahead. A warm blast of air struck them as they entered, and they both removed their gloves and opened the top buttons of their coats, laughing as they realised they mirrored each other's actions. The children's clothing department was on the second floor, so they made for the escalator. Bonnie was overwhelmed by the colours and people. It had been months since she had been in a large shop like this, and it was all a bit too much. She kept her eyes fixed straight ahead, concentrating on the escalator.

The children's department was vast, with a huge array of clothes to fit all ages, from babies to teens. Boys to the left, girls to the right. Babies at the front, teens towards the back of the store. Colours, patterns, shapes and sizes. It felt as if they were flying towards Bonnie, overpowering her senses. She wondered how parents managed to cope with a shop like this. She usually bought her girls' clothes from smaller stores. How would you cope if you had both boys and girls? You would have to walk up and down the whole floor, going from left to right to find what you wanted.

She turned to Mary, "I feel exhausted!" she said, laughing to make light of her rising panic. "So many things and colours, I don't know what to do."

Mary smiled, slipped her hand into Bonnie's elbow and began moving her towards the back of the store.

"Skye is ten, did you say?"

Bonnie nodded. "She'll be eleven in two months," she whispered.

Mary patted her arm. "Well, the clothes for girls of her age seem to be in this part of the store. Look. 'Girls 8 - 11 years' it says here."

Bonnie looked at the sign in surprise. Why, it was quite simple really! If you found the signs you would know where to look for what you wanted. How silly of her to get so worked up, when it was all so uncomplicated, when you looked at it the right way. She rubbed her hands over her face, taking a deep breath.

She walked forward, fingering the material of a blue dress, which would probably fit Skye. It was made of a thick fleecy material, which would be lovely and warm in the winter. A red flower was embroidered over the pocket on the skirt, a pattern which continued around the collar. It was lovely, and would look pretty on Skye. The blue was almost the exact same colour as her eyes. Bonnie looked at the price tag, which read £34.99. It seemed a lot of money to her, more than she would usually spend on a child's dress. But then, she reasoned, she hadn't bought anything for Skye for a long time. She picked the dress up off the rack, holding it by the hanger.

"I like this," she said quietly to Mary. "Do you think it would be silly of me to buy it for Skye? I could give it to her when she comes home. It will be nice and warm for the winter. If she hasn't been outside for months I expect she will feel the cold."

She realised that she was gabbling a bit senselessly, and stopped suddenly. Mary was smiling, her eyes kind. "Of course you should buy it if you think it will suit her. You're her mother, you know best about these things."

Her kind words brought tears to Bonnie's eyes, but she kept smiling as she dug around in her bag to find her purse. If she used her credit card it would be OK. It was meant for emergencies, but this felt important. Oh, what was the matter with her today? Her mind was jumping about all over the place. She wondered briefly if somebody had put something in her tea, but that was ridiculous. She had to assume it was nerves, although why this trip should be so nerve-wracking she couldn't begin to understand. She walked towards the counter. 'Please Pay Here'. It was simple really, she reminded herself, just follow the signs.

As she was paying for the dress, she felt Mary nudge her, and looked around in surprise. "The photo?" Mary whispered, "You were going to show the photo." Bonnie suddenly remembered the point of this trip, and opened her purse to find the photo of Skye which she carried around with her all the time now.

"Erm, I wondered," she began, as the shop assistant looked at her enquiringly, "have you seen this little girl? We think she might have been brought in here about two and a half months ago. She was wearing red jeans and a green T-shirt."

The assistant took the photo from her, looking at it for a moment and shaking her head. She then turned to her colleague and asked; "Emily, have you ever seen this little girl? Lady thinks she might have been brought in here about two or three months ago." Emily took the photo from her, holding it at the ends of her long-nailed fingers. She looked at it for longer than the first assistant, her lips pursed.

"You know, she does look familiar," she said, unaware of how her words caused Bonnie's heart to race. "I can't remember exactly when she came in, but I remember because she looked so worried. Her dad was holding her hand very tight, and she kept looking up at him as if she was worried about something. I can't remember what......" Her words trailed off as Bonnie gave a little moan before dropping into a faint.

Bonnie came to on a sofa in the staff room, a glass of water on a table beside her, and Mary sitting opposite her, looking terrified. The shop assistant, Emily, was next to Mary, and they had obviously been talking.

"Oh, Bonnie, are you all right?" Mary said, her voice filled with dismay, "We were beginning to wonder if we should call an ambulance."

Bonnie shook her head and struggled to a sitting position. She lifted the water to her lips with shaking hands, and took a cautious sip. "I'm all right," she croaked, trying to convince herself as much as the others. She looked at Emily. "I'm sorry for making such a fuss," she said, "has Mary explained things to you?"

Emily nodded. "I'm so sorry," she said, "obviously I had no idea. I've told your friend everything I remember, which isn't much more than I said to you before you fainted. I thought the man with her was her dad, but that she was worried about something."

"Can you remember anything about the man?" Bonnie asked.

"Not really, no. Sorry." Emily replied, "It was several months ago now."

When Bonnie had assured Emily and her supervisor that she was perfectly all right, thank you very much, she and Mary made their way out into the street. Bonnie took a deep breath of the cold winter air.

"I've never fainted before in my life," she mused.

"I don't suppose you've ever had such emotionally stressful things happen to you before either," Mary said. "Well, I think this shopping trip is over now."

Bonnie looked at her in surprise. "But..," she began.

"No buts," Mary said firmly, "I don't think we really need another experience like that, do you? You've learned that Skye came into this shop, but it hasn't really taught you anything you didn't already know. We'll go and eat some lunch somewhere, so you feel a bit stronger to drive, but then we're going home. No arguments." And Bonnie followed her meekly down the road, the bag with the precious dress in held firmly under her arm.

TWENTY SEVEN

Mary found a very dispirited Bonnie sitting at her kitchen table Friday morning. She was slumped over her mug of tea, her eyes downcast and her mouth drawn down at the corners.

"You look as if you have the weight of the world on your shoulders," Mary said, her tone gentle. Bonnie simply nodded. Mary poured herself a mug of tea and sat down opposite Bonnie. "Do you want to talk about what's on your mind?" she asked, "sometimes it helps to talk." She waited patiently as Bonnie rubbed at an invisible spot on the tablecloth before looking up at her.

"I feel such a fool," she began. "I came to Devon to find Skye, and I've achieved nothing. Tomorrow Dan and Summer are coming to take me home, and then what? How will I ever find Skye again?" Her eyes glistened with tears, but she continued, "I made you think that your next door neighbour was a kidnapper, and we spent days getting all stewed up about that, all for nothing. So it turns out he's just a sad little man trying to grow his own marijuana. Then yesterday was just the pits for me. Somehow thinking that if we went to Exeter, I'd find clues to what happened to Skye, and then just panicking like an idiot. I can't begin to imagine what that shop assistant must have thought of me, fainting like that! It's all been such a waste of time, and I've upset Summer by being away so long, and Dan's probably all cross with me, and I've done nothing. Nothing!"

"I wouldn't say it's nothing," Mary replied quietly. Bonnie looked up at her, eyebrows raised. "You have actually achieved quite a bit," Mary continued; "For a start, you've made me very happy. It has been a real pleasure getting to know you, and I've loved having you to stay. And as for Mr Ballard, well, maybe he wasn't the answer to our hopes, but you alerted me to the fact that something was wrong so I phoned the police. Who knows what would have happened if you hadn't? He could have died lying in his cellar with a broken back. He may not be a very nice man, but he doesn't deserve that." She reached across the table and held Bonnie's hand. "You are a remarkable woman, Bonnie Taylor, and don't you forget it."

Bonnie gave a little sob, and lowered her head onto her crossed arms. She cried for a few minutes, while Mary stroked her hair. Eventually she pulled herself together, and Mary got up to make some toast. As she lit the grill, she chatted about the things they had done and seen during the past week. Bonnie was reminded of Jenny, who Mary had introduced her to on her first day in the village.

"Perhaps we could go and see her today?" she suggested, "she seemed so nice."

"Yes," Mary said, "that would be nice; maybe we could go this afternoon. Oh, but Bonnie! I do wish Gladys would contact me." She turned to look at Bonnie, her face drawn into sad lines. "I do miss her. She was such a good friend to me before and we used to have such laughs together. I do wish I knew what had gone wrong."

"Perhaps it's nothing to do with you at all," Bonnie suggested, "Maybe she has a problem of her own that she doesn't want to talk about. I doubt very much if you've done anything to upset her, you're far too kind."

Mary smiled. "Thank you, Bonnie. Maybe it's her daft old son, Jim, who's causing her grief. It wouldn't surprise me."

"Yes, what is his problem?" Bonnie asked. "He looked terrified when we went to his house. I wonder if he had a woman in there and was worried you'd tell his wife."

Mary shouted with laughter at that, causing Bonnie to look at her with surprise.

"What's so funny about that?" she asked.

"Oh, Bonnie, Jim's never had one woman, let alone a wife and a woman on the side! Oh, the very idea of anybody finding him attractive kills me!" and she went off into further peals of laughter. "I thought I'd told you he wasn't married. Whatever made you think he was?"

Bonnie pondered this for a moment? Why had she been so sure that he had a wife? In fact, she had been convinced that he not only had a wife, but children too. She drew her mind back to the few moments they had stood at Jim's front door. What was it that had made her think of children? Was it the kicked paint on the front door? Or was it....

"Oh, dear God!" she said faintly. Mary looked at her in alarm. "Oh, God, oh, Mary, oh, dear God!"

She felt as if she was rushing down a dark tunnel, the walls surging in towards her. The light in the room seemed to change until she was peering through fog at the pinprick of light that was Mary. She licked her thick tongue around her lips, trying to draw enough moisture into her mouth to allow her to vocalise what she knew. A glass of water appeared in front of her eyes, and she took it from Mary, gulping the cold water gratefully. She tried to put the glass on the table, but kept missing, flailing around at the edge of the table until Mary took it from her.

Mary's face came into view as she knelt down in front of Bonnie. "Bonnie?" she asked, "what is it? You look so ill suddenly. Has something happened?"

Bonnie nodded. She took a few deep, shuddering breaths, locking eyes with Mary all the while.

"I saw something at Jim's house," she managed finally. Mary nodded encouragingly, so she persevered. "I knew that I somehow had the idea he was married, but I also thought that he had children, but didn't know why I thought that. I've just remembered what I saw that gave me that idea," she looked at Mary for courage as she dragged the words out. "He has a table in his hall. It's not very tidy there, is it?" Mary shook her head, waiting. "There was something under the table, on the floor, and I only just realised what it was. Mary, it was the ornament off Skye's sock! When she went missing she was wearing her favourite socks. They are white ankle socks, and sewn onto them is a little Scottie dog. She loves those socks. That little dog kept falling off, so I often had to sew it on again. And that's what is on the floor in his hall."

Mary was staring at her open mouthed. "But," she began, then stopped, bewildered.

"I know," Bonnie said. "There is only one explanation, isn't there? It must be Jim who has taken Skye, and those other girls I expect. Maybe Gladys has some idea of what he's done and that's why she won't see you?"

Mary remembered the day Gladys had seen the picture of Skye and her kidnapper on the notice board, and her bizarre reaction to it. She stood up now and unpinned the picture from the board, bringing it to the table and laying it gently before Bonnie. They looked intently at the fuzzy unfocused picture for a moment.

"It could be him," Mary said, horrified wonderment creeping into her voice. "But he's so mild, Bonnie! I know he's a bit of a misfit and not very bright, but why on earth would he kidnap children and keep them in his house? It doesn't make sense."

"I don't want to imagine what he wants them for," Bonnie said, her voice quiet and determined, "I just want to know what we do to get them back now that we know where they might be? I'll find out what went on later. I just want to get Skye back. Oh Mary! To think that we stood at his front door! If I had shouted loudly Skye might have heard me! Oh, she might have heard my voice anyway and wondered why I didn't take her home with me!"

"Bonnie, I don't think you actually spoke to him," Mary said. She was looking white and trembly, and Bonnie was worried for her friend. "What do you think we can do to make the police listen to me?" she asked, glancing vaguely out at the garden. "I'm a bit worried because they didn't really take much notice when I told them about Mr Ballard boarding up his windows, and they might just think I'm going round the village accusing every man I see!" She turned to look at her friend.

Mary nodded, lost in thought for a moment. Then suddenly she jerked out of her contemplation, and sat up straighter.

"You know, Bonnie," she began, "I think the only thing is for us to actually go to the police station where you reported Skye missing. They must have a record of what happened. And you do have some kind of proof, having seen the dog from Skye's sock. They must take some notice of that."

Bonnie was watching her carefully, drumming her fingers softly on the table.

"You must simply insist that somebody takes you seriously. We could refuse to leave the station until they do something. What was the name of that family liaison officer you knew?"

"Wendy Usher, but I think she thinks I've gone potty."

"It doesn't matter what she thinks," Mary said fiercely, "she has a duty to look into the matter. I'm sure she has."

"You're a good person to have on my side," Bonnie said, managing a small smile. "Come on then, let's get going, no time like the present!" And she jumped to her feet and headed for the door.

Twenty Eight

Bonnie was feeling the adrenalin rushing through her, making her want to put her foot to the floor and speed the car towards the Lynton police station. However, good sense told her that a few extra minutes were unlikely to change things very much for Skye, and it would be better to drive carefully in the icy conditions. Every traffic light seemed to be stuck on red, and she found herself impatiently revving the engine as she waited for lights to change.

As they drove past the signs for Lynmouth she thought about the days they had spent there last summer, and a new thought came to her, causing her to slam her foot on the brake, almost jerking Mary out of her seat.

"Sorry, Mary, sorry," she gasped, "but I just realised something. Do you remember when we were in the tea room with your friend Jenny and Jim walked past?" Mary nodded. "I said then that he reminded me of someone, and you two laughed and said it must be Richard Gere. Remember?" Again Mary nodded, but said nothing. "I've just realised where I'd seen him before. On the first full day of our holiday, two days before Skye disappeared, Skye and I were walking back to the cottage and a man on the other side of the river was walking along looking at us all the time. Did I tell you this before?" Another nod. "Well I'm as sure as it is possible to be that it was Jim. I think it was the way he walks as much as anything that reminded me. Do you think he could have been watching us to see if he could snatch Skye from me?"

"I think anything's possible now," Mary said. "When I saw that fuzzy picture on the television and again in the newspaper I thought he looked hauntingly familiar, but couldn't put my finger on who it was. I think as much as anything, that was because I just couldn't imagine Jim doing something so horrible, but now I wonder. I told you about Gladys' odd reaction when she saw I had that picture on my wall, and now I really do begin to think that she either knows or guesses what he's up to. I know she goes in and does some bits of cleaning for him, and it is likely that she's seen or heard something while she's been there. I am furious to think she might have been keeping quiet about something so horrible."

"Well, maybe she didn't know for sure, Mary. Perhaps she just had some suspicions about Jim, and when she saw the picture on your wall, she might have panicked."

They sat in silence for a few minutes; each lost in her own thoughts, before Bonnie started the car again and proceeded towards Lynton.

When they had reached Lynton and parked the car, Bonnie stood for a few moments outside the police station. It held so many unhappy memories for her and she really wanted to believe that things would now change, but she was afraid. What was she going to do if Wendy refused to listen to her? Or if they told her to come back next week?

Filling her lungs she ran her hands over her hair, trying to make herself look presentable then, squaring her shoulders she pushed open the door and entered. An older policeman was at the desk this time. Bonnie had to clear her throat a few times before she was able to speak.

"I'd like to speak to Wendy Usher please," she managed at last, "it is rather urgent."

"Is that right?" the policeman asked, looking her up and down. "And who shall I say is calling?"

"Bonnie Taylor," she replied, holding on to the desk to stop herself from shaking.

"Take a seat then, and I'll see if she is available."

Bonnie and Mary sat on the bench where Bonnie had waited on her last visit. It was warm in the station, and Bonnie soon had to remove her gloves and scarf. Her hands were visibly shaking, and she clasped them between her knees to try to control their tremor.

After a long wait Wendy appeared, looking a little flustered.

"How can I help you, Bonnie?" She asked.

"I have something important to tell you," Bonnie began. The door opened, and an elderly couple entered, a gust of cold wind blowing in with them. They went straight to the desk to enquire about a missing wallet. "Would it be possible to go somewhere a little more private?" Bonnie asked.

Wendy thought for a second, then said, "OK. Come this way. Is this your mother?" looking at Mary.

"Oh, no," Bonnie replied and proceeded to introduce Mary. They were led into a small office, which Bonnie assumed was Wendy's own, as there were photographs on the desk of her with a man. She wondered if he was Wendy's husband, or boyfriend. She had no idea if Wendy was married, she realised, although Wendy knew plenty about her life.

"What is the problem, Bonnie?" Wendy asked. Bonnie began to tell the story of Jim Walker, with occasional input from Mary. As they got to the part of the story where they went to Jim's front door, Wendy stopped them.

"Is there a point to this?" She asked. "Why are you telling me about this man?"

"Because the ornament off Skye's sock is under the table in his hall, and he has no children or wife and he acted really weird, as if he was scared that I was there and he looks like the man on the television who was with Skye and I remembered where I'd seen him before and it was in Lynmouth where he was following me and Skye along by the river." Bonnie practically shouted this all out at top speed, so afraid of not getting the chance to tell the most important part of her story while she had the chance. Wendy looked dumbfounded, and held her hands up to stall her.

"Slow down, Bonnie," she said, "try and tell me more slowly."

So she did. She explained it all as calmly as possible, from Jim's odd behaviour at his front door, to her realisation that she had seen Skye's scottie dog under his hall table. Wendy sat and listened, occasionally taking notes. When Bonnie had finished Wendy stood up.

"I need to talk to my superior about this, Bonnie," she said. "Can you sit here for a moment and I promise I'll be back?" Bonnie nodded. As the door closed behind her Bonnie and Mary looked at each other. Bonnie's cheeks were flushed, her lips white, her hands knotted so tightly in her lap that her knuckles were white.

"That didn't go too badly, I thought," Mary said, which caused Bonnie to giggle as she remembered her outburst.

"I told you she thinks I'm nutty," she whispered, "now I've gone and proved it." And they both giggled at the memory.

After a few minutes Wendy returned with an older man in plain clothes. He was introduced as DI Langton, and he asked to be told the story. He sat patiently and listened as Bonnie told her story again, aiming to be as succinct as possible this time. DI Langton took notes, scratching his head with his pen from time to time. He was a tall good looking man with long muscular legs, and a head of greying brown hair. Bonnie felt drawn to him, that she could trust him. When she had finished her tale, he crossed his arms and sat looking at her for a moment with his piercing green eyes.

"You're sure about all this, Bonnie?" he asked, scrutinising her face as she nodded in reply.

"OK, then," he said, standing up. "What we need to do is get some men round there to talk to this man and have a look around his house."

Bonnie felt her heart racing. He was going to do something! Someone was actually going to do something about what she had seen. Did this mean that DI Langton actually believed her? She looked at him, her mouth agape.

"You're going to go and see him? Today?" she asked.

"Of course," he replied, "you are Skye's mother. If you think you have good reason to believe that your daughter is being held at this man's house then it is our duty to look into it. Having part of Skye's sock in his house is reason enough to arrest him on suspicion while we check his house. Don't look so worried," this last in a more gentle tone, "I'm sure everything will work out well in the end. If you and your friend would like to wait here we'll get someone to bring you a hot drink, and we'll come straight back here afterwards to let you know how things have progressed."

"No!" Bonnie protested, standing up so suddenly that she knocked her chair over. "I won't stay here! I want to be there when you bring Skye out. I won't interfere, and I won't try to come into the house or anything, but I must be there."

DI Langton considered Bonnie for a few moments, tapping his pen on his teeth as he did so. "Very well," he said at last, "but you have to do as you are asked."

Bonnie nodded eagerly. "Anything," she gasped, "I'll do whatever you say, just please don't make me stay here."

They were led out to the car park where they were ushered into a squad car and seated in the back with Wendy. A policeman drove the car, and they were followed by an unmarked car which held DI Langton and another plain clothes policeman.

It seemed a very long drive back to Lynhoe. Bonnie wanted this moment to be over, but was at the same time filled with dread at the thought of arriving at Jim's house. What would they find there? She felt as if the police car was driving in slow motion through the frozen streets.

"I wish it was tomorrow," she muttered to Mary. "I just want to wake up and have this whole nightmare over and done with." Mary reached over and patted her hand.

"It soon will be, dear," she said.

Time suddenly seemed to speed up again as Bonnie began to recognise landmarks. Here they were driving past the road where Julie Davenport lived. She wondered how she was feeling today? And there was Mary's dear, sweet, homely cottage. And here again was the end of the road where they were turning, and Gladys' house. And there, of course, was Jim's unkempt house next door. Now they were pulling up outside, and Bonnie put her hands over her face, unable to bear what might or might not happen in the next moments.

TWENTY NINE

The car pulled in outside Gladys' house, the unmarked car drawing up behind it. The police all got out of their cars and stood around talking for a moment, before Wendy returned to the car Bonnie and Mary were in, and got into the front seat, turning around to look at them.

"You must stay in the car for now. Can I have your promise that you won't do anything without my say-so, no matter what happens?"

Bonnie nodded, her heart racing, the heat rising to her cheeks. No matter what happens! Whatever did Wendy expect them to see? She turned to look out of the window, afraid, but wanting to know what was going on. The three policemen, one in uniform, two in plain clothes, were walking up Jim's front path. They knocked, and after a few moments the door was opened. She could not see Jim's face from this distance in the dark of the afternoon; she just gained an impression of a white horrified face in the doorway. Then the face disappeared and the police followed, and all was silent. There was not even one person out on the street, although she had the impression that curtains were twitching up and down the road.

There was a digital clock on the dashboard of the police car. Its numbers slid slowly through the minutes, and still there was silence from Jim's house. Bonnie could not take her eyes from his front door, wondering what was taking place behind its grubby exterior.

Suddenly the silence was broken by the sound of Wendy's walkie talkie blaring into life. Bonnie jumped in her seat, aware that Mary beside her also started. Wendy got out of the car, closing the door behind her and walking a few paces along the road until they could not hear what she said. Bonnie looked round towards Mary, their eyes locking, bolts of fear passing from one to the other.

The minutes continued to tick by. Bonnie's heart beat with the cadence of a speeded up metronome, her breath coming in shallow gasps. Wendy reappeared at the car window, opening the door and putting her head in.

"I need to go into the house for a minute," she said, "This is PC Gibbs. He'll stay with you till I get back. OK?" She smiled at them as she indicated the tall young policeman beside her. Bonnie had not been aware of the third police car which was now parked behind the unmarked car, so was startled to see a new face. PC Gibbs climbed into the front passenger seat, and Wendy made her way up Jim's front path, knocking on the door, which was opened almost immediately. PC Gibbs smiled at Mary and Bonnie, then turned and looked out of the window.

It was cold inside the car. Bonnie pulled her gloves out of her pocket, easing them over her frozen fingers. Her teeth were chattering, although whether with cold or nerves she was unsure. She remembered the night Skye had disappeared, and how her teeth had chattered then, even though it was a warm night. She pulled her scarf tighter around her neck, and as she looked up again, saw movement in the road outside. Some people were walking up the road, stopping outside Jim's front gate. Peering through the gloom she tried to see who they were. There were two men and two women, talking to yet another policeman, who seemed to be standing guard at the gate.

With a jolt of shock, Bonnie recognised one of the women - it was Julie Davenport - Molly's mother! Was that other woman Lauren's mother? She wondered. And what about the two men? Could they be the fathers of the missing girls? She wondered how they knew what was happening. Had word spread so soon? Or, shocking thought, had the police brought them here? Surely they would only do that if they knew for certain the girls were here?

"Why are they here?" she asked PC Gibbs.

"No idea," he said, his voice devoid of expression. "I know it's hard, Mrs Taylor, but do try to be patient."

Patient! How would he feel if it was his daughter in there? Or not. Bonnie was fuming. She put her hand on the door lever, preparing to go and join the other parents at the gate, but PC Gibbs turned to her, saying,

"Please be patient just a little longer, Mrs Taylor. You promised to stay in the car, and I don't want to have to force the issue."

Bonnie was shocked at the implication, and a vision of herself fighting with PC Gibbs raced through her mind. Her face flushed with embarrassment.

She turned once again to look at the street outside, leaning her hot face against the cool glass of the window. Would this day ever end?

And then there was movement outside. The people at the gate stirred, and she realised that Jim's front door was opening. She sat up straighter in her seat, reaching beside her to grasp Mary's hand, hearing her gasp, and remembering her painful arthritis. "Sorry," she muttered, holding the hand more loosely. The door opened wider. If only she could see better! She craned forward to see who was coming out, recognising Wendy's dark head, and then seeing that she was not alone. Wendy was holding two children by the hand. Girl children. Bonnie let out a moan, and Mary put her arm round her. Wendy and the two children walked up to the figures waiting at the gate, gently handing Molly and Lauren over to their parents, who fell on their daughters, hugging and kissing them, crying on to their heads.

Behind them, Jim's front door quietly swung closed.

***

The cellar door creaked open. Skye sat very still. She knew it was day time, and the door had never been opened in the day. Well, only twice. The first time, of course, was the day when Buddy had brought her here, and the second time had been just two weeks ago, when he had brought the other two girls here. She had been sitting quietly that day, re-reading 'Five on a Treasure Island', and had felt worried when the door suddenly opened, and she could hear Buddy whispering, and lots of footsteps on the stairs. She had looked up, surprised and a bit scared to see not just Buddy, but also two girls about her age. She didn't know what to say, so sat silent, knowing that eventually someone would speak.

It was Buddy who spoke first, "Look Skye! We've got some friends to play with!" was what he said to her surprise. "You were right about not having enough people to play proper games, so I've brought Molly and Lauren to play with us. Now we can really play Cluedo!"

Skye was horrified. 'He's really mad!' she thought, suddenly feeling quite frightened. What if she'd said she wanted to play football? Would he have gone and got ten people to play with them? Or twenty-one so they could have two teams? She stifled a nervous giggle, putting her hand over her mouth. Those two girls must wonder what he was talking about.

"I'll just go and get a few things you'll need," Buddy said, and skipped off up the stairs, sounding really happy. The two girls stood and looked at Skye. They looked scared, but also a bit cross, as if they thought this was her fault.

"Hello," Skye said, her voice quiet. "My name's Skye. I've been here quite a long time now, since the summer."

One of the girls opened her eyes wide. "Are you that girl that disappeared off the rocks at Lynmouth?" she asked. Skye nodded.

"Wow!" the girl said, "everyone thought you were dead! Then they saw you on the television and knew you had to be alive somewhere but no-one knew where. Was that Mr Walker with you on the telly?"

Skye had no idea what she was talking about. "I've never been on television," she said, confusion showing in her voice. "I've been here in the cellar all the time. Who's Mr Walker?"

"But you were seen by, umm, I think it was Exeter Cathedral," the other girl piped up. "They were doing a news thing about the Cathedral, and you and a man walked past. Your mum saw it on the telly and then she was on the telly asking the man to bring you home. Was it Mr Walker?"

Skye's eyes filled with tears at the thought of her mummy on the television, asking Buddy to bring her home. "It must have been the day we went out shopping," she managed to say, "It's the only time I've been out. He made me hide in the car, and we went to this big town and bought some winter clothes. Is that his name then, Mr Walker? I thought it was just Buddy."

"Buddy! No, that's not a real name," the second girl said. "I don't know his first name, but he is Mr Walker. He works in the post office. What did he mean about games?"

Skye tried to explain, but realised that her explanations sounded a bit sad. She recognised that sitting upstairs playing board games with Buddy (Mr Walker) was really pathetic, but she had had no choice. Molly and Lauren sat down on her mattress, introducing themselves. Molly started to cry.

"Will he keep us here too?" she asked, "I want to go home. My mum will be wondering where I am."

"I don't know," Skye had said carefully. She really hoped not. She wished Buddy would just get bored with them and send them home. She wanted more than ever to see her family again, and she was beginning to think she would never get home now.

But now the cellar door was opening during the day again. She looked at Molly and Lauren, sitting on their mattresses next to hers, and they looked back at her. They all looked really scared, wondering what was going to happen now.

Feet came down the stairs, followed by an unfamiliar face.

"Hello, girls," the man said, sounding a bit surprised. Then Skye understood suddenly - the man was wearing a police uniform! She stood up.

"Hello," she said, "My name's Skye Taylor. This is Molly and Lauren. Have you come to take us home?"

THIRTY

Wendy walked over to where Bonnie sat shaking in the car. She bent down and opened the door.

"Come on, Bonnie," she said, her voice kind and gentle. Bonnie shook her head. She didn't want to go and see Molly and Lauren with their parents. Of course, she was really glad they were all back together, but it only hurt her more to see those girls back with their families.

But Wendy was smiling at her and holding out her hand. "Don't you want to come and see Skye? She's coming out in just a moment."

Bonnie heard a strange noise, and realised it was coming from her mouth. A sound somewhere between a moan and a scream. Her legs would not do as she commanded, and Wendy had to half drag her from the car. Mary followed behind, plucking ineffectually at her coat sleeve. They made their way towards the gate, where Molly and Lauren and their families were still clustered. Julie Davenport broke away from the group, recognising Bonnie, and hurrying forwards to hug her.

"Thank you, Bonnie," she gasped, "Thank you so much! If it wasn't for you we wouldn't have the girls back yet. They told us that Skye is in there, and she's been lovely to them." Bonnie hugged her back, holding on tightly for a moment as she felt the ground giving way beneath her. Skye was truly coming back to her now! This pain had all been worthwhile after all.

She turned to Wendy. "Why isn't Skye out yet?" she asked.

"She wanted to say goodbye to Mr Walker, and to reassure us that he is not really a bad man." She smiled. "That's quite a remarkable little girl you have there, Bonnie." Bonnie simply stood and looked at her, tears coursing down her face, her whole body wracked with shivers.

And then Wendy walked away, back up the path. The door opened and two policemen came out, Jim Walker handcuffed between them, his eyes cast down towards the path. He did not look at any of the parents as he was led away into the waiting police car. And the door opened again, and Wendy reappeared with another little girl who looked a lot like Skye. So much so that Bonnie knew now that it truly was her baby, not some wraith from a dream. Skye looked up then and caught sight of Bonnie. Her eyes opened wide and she pulled away from Wendy, running up the path towards her mother, as Bonnie ran to meet her.

"Mummy! Oh, Mummy!" she cried, as Bonnie echoed her cries with, "Skye! Oh, Skye!"

And then they were together, Skye was in her arms, holding on so tightly that Bonnie knew they would never be parted again. She put her hand to Skye's face, marvelling at the reality of holding her so close, kissing her dear little face again and again.

Together they walked back down the path, through the crowds who had appeared from somewhere. Together they climbed into the back of the police car as Bonnie reached out for Mary, who was holding back, tears running down her lovely face, shaking her head in acknowledgement that mother and daughter should be left alone together. Together they fastened their seat belts as the car pulled away from the kerb, their arms wrapped around each other, Bonnie's tears falling on to Skye's grubby hair.

As the car sped away Skye finally looked up at her mother, her face streaked with tears and grime. "It's really you, isn't it Mummy? Not just another dream?" her little voice shook with fear.

"It's really, truly me darling. We're back together now, forever. I promise not to let you go again."

Skye began to sob then, her head on Bonnie's shoulder, her tears wetting her coat, and Bonnie held her gently but tightly, rocking her softly as she had done when she was a baby.

***

There was a brief knock at the door, then it was quickly opened and Dan's secretary put her head in. "I'm really sorry to bother you, Dan," she said, "but there are two policemen here and they say it's really urgent that they speak to you."

Dan nodded, and stood up behind his desk as John Chambers, their family liaison officer entered, followed by a man in police uniform.

Dan shook hands with them, wondering just what he had done to warrant this intrusion at work.

"Hello, Dan," John Chambers said, "I have some good news for you." Dan raised his eyebrows, but said nothing, waiting for the other man to continue. "Your wife seems to have done a remarkable bit of detection work, and found out where your daughter, Skye, and the other two girls, Lauren and Molly, were being held. We have arrested the man responsible, and your wife is at this moment on her way to the local hospital with Skye, so that she can be checked over by a police doctor. We would like you to come with us. We have a plane waiting at Southend Airport to take you to Exeter to meet them."

Dan became aware that he was standing with his mouth foolishly hanging open, and he hastily shut it. "Bonnie found Skye?" he repeated, unable to believe his ears.

"Yes. Well, she didn't exactly go in and get her herself, but she did the right thing and came to us. We went to the man's house and found the children there. Apparently unharmed," he added hurriedly.

Dan could think of nothing to say to that. Bonnie had actually done what she had set out to do! He had always thought his wife was pretty remarkable, but he hadn't expected her to really be able to find Skye. He sat down, afraid his legs would no longer hold him.

"Dan?" John was asking, "we need to go now to get the plane so you can meet them at the hospital."

Dan stood up, then remembered something. "What about Summer? We can't leave her here alone. Can we go and fetch her from school?"

"Of course, if we hurry," John replied, and with that Dan hurried, grabbing his coat from the back of the door and his briefcase from under the desk.

At the grammar school it took a little while until Dan was allowed to see Summer. She listened in open mouthed surprise, tears flooding her eyes, as he told her the story John had just recounted to him.

"Come on, love, get your things and we'll go and see Skye and Mum. We don't need to wait till tomorrow now!" And Summer ran off, returning a few minutes later with her coat under her arm and her bag flung carelessly over her shoulder.

On the way to the airport Summer kept asking; "Are they sure it's Skye they've found?" When John answered in the affirmative she said, "so Mum was right all along? Skye was still alive somewhere and nobody believed her." She was quiet for a few minutes before adding, "Poor Skye. Poor Mum." Dan put his arm around her, and she leaned into him as the car sped towards the airport.

All went surprisingly smoothly at the airport - the police had arranged everything for them. All they had to do was board the small aeroplane and within minutes it had taken off. Summer looked down at her home town spread out below her as the plane banked round. There was the sea, with the pier reaching out into the estuary like a ruler, straight and long. She watched the little houses, wondering if she would be able to make out their house, or her school, but all too soon they were up above the clouds and there was no more to see. She sat back in her seat, waiting impatiently for the plane to begin its descent to Exeter airport.

Dan chatted to John about the police investigation and where Skye had been found, but discovered that he knew little more than he had already told Dan.

They arrived in Exeter far sooner than Summer had thought they would. "That's the way to travel," Dan said smiling, as they made their way off the plane. "It takes at least 4 hours to drive, but less than an hour by air. Shame we can't get our own private plane!" Summer thought he must be nervous to be chattering so much. It wasn't like him normally.

There was a police car waiting outside the airport, and they sped away to the hospital. Everything became a blur as they were whisked past reporters, through doors and down corridors, until Summer felt completely lost. But then it all stopped. The local policeman who had been leading their charge through the hospital came to a halt outside a door that had a sliding notice which read 'occupied'. He knocked, and the door was opened by a frowning woman with wavy brown hair. When she learned who they were however, her face broke into a beautiful smile and she held the door open, ushering Summer and Dan into the room.

Bonnie was sitting on a chair, turning to face them, her face all blotchy from crying, but a huge smile lighting it up. And on her lap was Skye. Little, lost Skye, who had been brought back from the dead. She turned her head and saw them, then held out her arms saying; "Daddy! Summer! Hello! Oh, I've missed you all so much!" And with that she stood up and rushed towards them, and suddenly all four of them were tangled in one huge, warm embrace, everybody's tears mingled together, their arms locked around each other, and the nightmare began to fade away.

THIRTY ONE

The wavy haired woman introduced herself as Sheila Plackett, a child psychologist who worked at Exeter Hospital, but also helped the police. She explained that she needed to talk to Skye about her experiences while she was away from her family. Wendy Usher was seated in the corner of the room, a notebook in her hand.

"I don't want to take up too much of your time today," she assured them, looking at the family of four who had insisted on squeezing themselves onto two chairs in order that they could all be in physical contact with Skye. "I realise you all need some time together, and Skye can talk more to a psychologist when you return home. But for now, I just briefly need to know where you've been, and what you've been doing for the past five months," she smiled at Skye encouragingly.

"I've been in Buddy's cellar," Skye replied. "He kept me there most of the time. But in the evenings he would bring me upstairs to the living room to play with me."

Bonnie felt her stomach lurch sickeningly at these words, revolting images trying to force their way into her brain. She struggled against the nausea which was shifting against her throat, until she focused on what Skye was saying.

"He would make food that was kind of like party food most of the time, and we would play board games, like scrabble and monopoly and stuff like that. He never let me watch television or listen to the radio, but sometimes he would let me have a bath upstairs if I promised to be quiet." She smiled round at her mother. "I remembered to wash my hair in the bath, Mum."

Bonnie's sore eyes filled with yet more tears. "You're such a good girl," she whispered, kissing Skye's upturned face.

"He had some books on a shelf on the landing, and when I looked they were nearly all Famous Five books, and he let me read them. Sometimes we would talk about the books. Buddy said he always wanted to be Julian, and I wanted to be George, so we would talk about their adventures." She leaned back against Bonnie then, yawning widely.

"It's been a long day, hasn't it?" Sheila asked. Skye nodded, her eyes drooping.

"I'll let you go now," Sheila continued, "but I'd be grateful if you would come back tomorrow so we can talk a little bit more, just to see how Skye is coping. She's had a lot to cope with for such a young girl. It seems that she has coped marvellously so far." She was smiling at them all, when Skye suddenly sat up straight on Bonnie's lap.

"You mustn't think Buddy's a bad man!" she almost shouted. "He never did anything horrible to me. I know he could have hurt me or anything but he didn't. I was a bit worried when he brought Lauren and Molly, 'cos I thought he must be really mad to do that, but he isn't a bad man. Just a bit stupid," she finished quietly.

238

When they left Sheila's office the family felt a bit lost. "What shall we do now?" Dan asked.

"Oh! I really think we should phone Mary. She'll want to know where we are, and that you and Summer are here," Bonnie realised. John Chambers, who had been waiting outside the door, gave them his mobile phone, saying he would arrange to have them driven wherever they wanted to go once they left the hospital.

Bonnie rang Mary, who must have been sitting on top of the telephone, she answered so quickly. They were unable to speak for a moment, both crying into the phone, listening to each other's sobs and gulps.

"Mary, oh, Mary, thank you so much for all your help! We've really, truly got our Skye back now! And Dan and Summer are here too, they were brought in an aeroplane! I'd like them to meet you some time, but we need to think about where to go tonight and we'll come and see you in the morning." Bonnie was gabbling aimlessly into the receiver, while Dan stood near her smiling, his arms around Skye and Summer.

"Oh, Bonnie!" Mary managed at last, "Can't you all come and stay here tonight? It will be a bit of a squash, but you can all be together."

Bonnie relayed this to Dan, who nodded. They soon found themselves once more in a police car, speeding back towards Lynhoe. Skye fell asleep, her head in Bonnie's lap, an arm reaching out to hold Summer's hand. Dan, in the front seat, sat turned awkwardly towards them for almost the entire journey, unwilling to take his eyes off Skye, afraid she would disappear again if he looked away.

239

At Mary's cottage, introductions out of the way, they crammed themselves around the kitchen table to eat the roast dinner Mary had prepared for them. Everybody kept their attention on Skye, watching her every move, as if they had never seen a child eat dinner before. Bonnie sat gloriously close to her, her left thigh touching Skye's bony right knee. After dinner a bath was run for Skye, who admitted that it had been some days since Buddy had allowed her to have a bath.

"It was more difficult after the other girls came," she explained. "There were too many of us to be able to have baths very often. I think he was a bit worried we'd make too much noise and someone would hear." She allowed Bonnie to wash her hair for her, and afterwards was wrapped in a huge fluffy towel and sat on Dan's lap in front of the fire to drink hot chocolate.

"What am I going to wear?" she asked suddenly, "all my clothes are in the cellar!"

"Those are not your real clothes," Bonnie said, "Your own clothes are at home in your bedroom. You can wear one of my T-shirts to bed tonight." Then she remembered the fleecy dress she had bought in Exeter, yesterday but many lifetimes ago, and ran up to the bedroom, returning with the bag, which she handed to Skye.

Skye pulled the dress out of the bag, smiling with wonder, as if she had never seen a new dress before. "It's lovely!" she said, "thanks Mum!"

They all slept that night squashed together in the bed Bonnie had been sleeping in. Summer had insisted she was happy to sleep on a blow-up bed on the floor, but soon crept into the crowded double bed, where Skye was between her parents, and Summer snuggled up next to Bonnie. It was uncomfortable, but wonderful. Nobody slept very well, but nobody minded very much. They were a family again, their arms tangled together across Skye, their breath mingling on her face. Every hour or so Skye awoke briefly, reached up to touch Bonnie's face, then fell asleep again, smiling.